RIDE A DANCING HORSE

RIDE A DANCING HORSE

"Ride A Dancing Horse
*is like boarding a carousel... a wonderful spin
through the world of Andalusian horses and their
high-stepping ways. But this elegant background is deceiving,
because it's rife with intrigue and very real peril. The hero, Diego,
smolders through the pages, while the heroine, Kelly,
tries to lead him through his sorrow and distrust.
It's a ride you'll hope will never end!"*

—*Carolyn Banks*
Author of **Murder Well Bred**

...Kelly crept as close as she dared to the barn door, the heavy smoke beginning to choke her even from there. "Diego!" she called, straining her throat. "Get out of there, before—"

More ragged hoofbeats warned her to stand clear, just before Hidalgo sprang through the opening. A fringe of flame trailed from his flowing mane, but Diego still held his lead rope.

"Alonzo, the hose—!" Diego yelled, his voice raw.

Felipe's father aimed the burst of water briefly at the stallion's neck. He doused the burning mane, but unfortunately startled the high-strung animal even more. Hidalgo rear sharply, flinging Diego to the ground, and bolted free.

Trying to get to Diego, Kelly found herself face-to-face with the charging stallion. Remembering how Diego had stopped Belleza, Kelly threw her arms wide. For a second, she thought Hidalgo might run right over her, anyway...

ALSO BY EILEEN WATKINS
(Writing as E. F. Watkins)

Black Flowers
Dance With The Dragon

RIDE A DANCING HORSE

BY

EILEEN WATKINS

AMBER QUILL PRESS, LLC
http://www.amberquill.com

RIDE A DANCING HORSE
AN AMBER QUILL PRESS BOOK

Amber Quill Press, LLC
http://www.amberquill.com

Layout and Formatting provided by: ElementalAlchemy.com

PUBLISHED IN THE UNITED STATES OF AMERICA

For Anne-Marie,
who's listened to lots of "horse talk" during
our 30-plus years of friendship;
and in memory of Brenda,
my own "Gitano."

CHAPTER 1

The fence around the riding ring needed a fresh coat of paint, but Kelly rested her fingers against it respectfully. To her, it might have been the velvet rope around a museum exhibit, or the apron of a prestigious stage. The performance taking place beyond the wooden rails both fascinated and intimidated her.

I shouldn't be here, she told herself. *I'll never pull this off. I don't know what ever made me think I could!*

Inside the ring, a man with a bronzed profile right off a Spanish doubloon sat ramrod straight in his saddle. The stallion upon which he rode also looked like something out of a romantic legend—steel-gray and dappled with a thousand white starbursts, silver mane rippling almost to his knees, magnificent tail sweeping the ground. Responding to invisible cues from his rider, he pranced in slow motion across the ring in an ideal, classical *passage.*

An Andalusian—the traditional horse of the Spanish aristocracy. Kelly had seen such horses in books, but never in person.

Except for the man's modern riding clothes, he might have been performing in some royal court in eighteenth-century Spain, instead of practicing his skills alone on a ranch in present-day Southern California.

Despite the warm May breeze that ruffled her short, auburn hair, Kelly felt frozen in place, unable to either retreat or follow through on her original plan.

I'm an imposter. Sure, I've ridden dressage, but not at this guy's

1

level. He'll figure that out in an instant. He'll never hire me!

Once horse and rider reached the center of the ring, the stallion high-stepped in place, in the movement Kelly recognized as the *piaffe*. He bent his hind legs deeply and lifted them sharply, in a crisp one-two rhythm she knew was both difficult to achieve and highly rated in the show ring.

Observing the rider, Kelly felt as if she were watching a fine Shakespearean actor rehearse his lines on an empty stage. She dreaded the moment when he might call her up there to play her role—a part for which she felt ill prepared. She told herself she should walk straight back to her dark green Blazer, before the man even spotted her, and drive away from Rancho Villaneuva as fast as she could.

Then she remembered how badly she needed this job.

I'll have to play it smart. This guy doesn't know a thing about me, where I come from, my experience or lack of it. I'll just try to keep it that way! After all, it won't be the first time I've had to bluff my way out of a tight spot.

Kelly assumed the rider before her was the owner of the ranch, Diego Villanueva. She'd imagined an older man, but this one couldn't be more than thirty-five.

He should have spotted her by now, but he gave no sign of it. He continued to work the horse while sitting immobile as a statue. His black hair boiled back from his high forehead as if from the intensity of his concentration. The muscles of his forearms swelled below the short sleeves of his knit shirt, but other than that, no sign of his efforts showed. Even his legs in their high, black leather boots barely nudged the horse's sides.

At two p.m., the sun had built up its full strength. Kelly had to stretch a little to see over the top rail, and her shoulders baked in her long-sleeved cotton shirt. She shrugged out of her khaki vest and hung it by one armhole on the nearest fencepost, her eyes still on the rider. Dressage was often defined as ballet on horseback, and the way these two performed, it lived up to that description.

She noticed one odd thing, though. Despite the grace of his performance, the rider wore an expression that went beyond serious, crossing the line to somber. He seemed isolated in his own world, and from his face, Kelly guessed it wasn't a pleasant place to be.

Now the dappled gray stallion lifted and folded his front legs, not in a wild rear, but in a controlled *levade*. He sat back on his powerful haunches for several seconds, before dropping gracefully to all fours again.

Just then, a gust of the lurking wind caught Kelly's vest. It lifted from the fencepost, and scudded across the outdoor ring with a noisy hiss.

The stallion flew up into the air again, this time of his own accord. His rider barked a sharp reproach in Spanish, and brought the horse back under control. Diego Villanueva finally acknowledged Kelly's presence with an angry glare, made particularly effective by the blackness of his eyes.

"S-sorry!" Kelly ducked through the wide space between the fence rails in an effort to retrieve the vest, but the rider held up a hand to warn her back. He swung lightly out of his saddle to pick up the offending garment himself.

Once he held the reins securely under the stallion's chin, Kelly approached, cheeks burning, to reclaim her vest. "I thought it was safe enough on the fencepost."

The dark man, who stood about six feet tall, slapped his mount's neck in an affectionate reprimand. "Hidalgo has been looking for an excuse to misbehave today."

And I, unfortunately, gave him one! Kelly feared she'd undermined her credibility already. She noticed the rider's royal-blue polo shirt clung in a few dark spots, a testament to how hard he actually had been working. She couldn't help observing also that the chest beneath seemed nicely muscled, as did the thighs in those tight-fitting gray breeches. Shaking off her nerves, she put out a hand and introduced herself. "You must be *Señor* Villanueva. I'm Kelly Sheridan. I'm interviewing for the job. Assistant trainer?"

This information seemed to confuse, almost annoy him. "Oh. Was that today?"

She nodded. "I made the appointment Monday with Helga, your stable manager. I hope she told you?"

"I'm sure she did. I've just...had other things on my mind."

Both the purity of Diego's Spanish accent and the formality of his manner suggested an aristocratic background. His features also seemed molded by centuries of Spanish nobility, straight of nose and cleft of chin. Kelly wondered what it must be like to tan that deeply and evenly, rather than burning and freckling the way she did.

Diego looked her over, too, and cleared his throat. "If you don't mind my asking, how old—?"

Kelly was used to it. Because of her petite build, boyishly cropped,

3

wavy hair, wide, hazel eyes and upturned nose, people often mistook her for a college kid. "I'm twenty-seven."

At his master's side, the dappled stallion chewed the bit and rolled one dark eye towards Kelly from beneath the heavy silver forelock, as if he had doubts about her, too.

"What a beautiful animal!" Moving slowly, she patted the thick, arched neck, damp from the horse's exertions.

Diego softened at this praise, and the corners of his shapely mouth finally lifted in a smile. "Hidalgo is our prize. He can do even more than what you saw, when he keeps his mind on his business. He is *alta escula!*"

Kelly had heard the French version of this phrase more often than the English, but knew it referred to a horse trained to the highest level of dressage, such as those who performed with the Spanish Riding School.

Still acting distracted, almost uninterested, Diego finally asked the question Kelly had been dodging. "Well, as long as you're here…What experience have you had training horses?"

She launched into her practiced spiel. "I've specialized in dressage for the last six years. I studied with a protégé of Robert Dover's. I'm sure you've heard of him—he rode with the U.S. Equestrian Team."

Diego nodded slowly. "He trains on the east coast, doesn't he?"

"That's right. He's originally from New Jersey, like me." Kelly could see her name-dropping had impressed Diego, so she forged ahead. "I brought a Thoroughbred mare up to second level, and won first and second prizes with her at a lot of A-rated shows. We never scored under seventy percent. I can give you my resumé…" She made a show of fumbling in her backpack. "Darn, I must've left it in the car."

With an air of impatience, Diego shrugged. "You can give it to me later. I don't care so much about that. I've interviewed people with all kinds of awards and referrals who can't even sit correctly! To me, the most important thing is whether you can ride." He nodded towards the larger of the two white stucco barns, roofed in red tile. "Find Helga, ask her to give you a horse, and come back out here."

"Great," Kelly told him. "Thanks!"

With a sigh of relief, she told herself she'd cleared the first hurdle. Even if her prospective boss seemed less than enthusiastic about her tryout.

On her way to the main barn, Kelly passed a scenic patch of garden dominated by a spiky yucca plant, with various types of cacti grouped at its base. The plants should've been in flower around this time, but they badly needed watering. Some thought and effort had gone into the original landscaping of the ranch, she reflected, but now things looked overgrown and parched.

The barn interior provided blessed relief from the heat and dust outside. Skylights filtered the bright sunshine to a soft shimmer. Kelly savored the familiar, warm smell of hay and horses mingled together.

To either side stretched rows of roomy box stalls. Iron bars on top allowed her to glimpse the occupants, and vice versa.

More Andalusians. They differed from other breeds mainly in their stocky, powerful bodies, muscular, arched necks and dignified, Roman noses. The brass nameplates on the first three stalls identified the occupants as mares—Paloma, Duquesa and Contessa.

From the fourth stall came soft, coaxing phrases in a German accent. Kelly recognized the same female voice she'd heard on the phone when she made her appointment. Inside the stall, she found a woman in denim shorts trying to lure a foal out from behind his mother's dappled gray legs.

"How old is he?" Kelly asked, through the half-open door.

Helga glanced up with a wide, creased grin. "Just two weeks. We're trying to handle him as much as possible, to get him used to people, but he's still pretty shy."

"He's adorable!" Kelly said, as the nearly-black foal peered out at them with huge eyes.

Helga straightened to her full height, a good four inches taller than Kelly's. She wore a red "Barn Goddess" T-Shirt and a matching elastic hairband to hold back her graying bob. She offered her rawboned hand; her clasp was almost as strong as Diego's. Her German accent, however, sounded less pronounced than his Spanish one, and Kelly assumed she'd lived in America longer.

"You must be the girl who called about the job. Have you talked to the boss?"

"Just did. He wants you to put me on a horse."

Helga laughed. "Well, you have a wide choice. Let me introduce you to our family. You've met Esperanza and her baby Paco…" She closed their stall, and proceeded to one that housed a dark gray mare with a chiseled head and a regal attitude. "This is Belleza, our beauty— but I wouldn't recommend her for your tryout! Our boys are down here." She stopped in front of a nameplate that read Fantasmo, and clucked. A white gelding put his big nose up to the bars, his heavy forelock fanning over his eyes. His snowy coat told Kelly he must be one of the senior citizens, because gray horses lightened with age.

At the next stall, Helga explained, "This is Turi, our little bear." A tall, brown colt who looked about two years old peered out at them with a bright, mischievous expression. "I think you'll want to ride Gitano, our gypsy."

Kelly, who knew little Spanish, felt grateful that at least his name didn't translate as Psycho Killer. When Helga slid open the stall door, the gelding turned around and stretched his nose toward Kelly.

She understood instantly why they'd called him Gitano. He had the most unusual coloring she'd ever seen. She supposed he was technically a flea-bitten gray, his pale body lightly peppered with brown, but his nose, lower legs, mane and tail all shaded to a rich bronze, resembling the points on a Siamese cat. Eyes calm and ears pricked forward, he radiated friendliness. Kelly patted his big, round cheek and told him, "Gitano, you're gorgeous!"

"Beautiful to ride, too," Helga half-whispered, as if it were a secret. "Can you tell I want you to get this job?"

Kelly laughed. "You must really need the help!"

"I do. We have a Mexican family, the Martinezes, to keep up the house and grounds, and the boy helps in the stable before and after school. But for actually working the horses, there's just Diego and me now. It's too much—some of these guys haven't been ridden in a week."

"The job comes with housing on the premises, right?"

Helga nodded. "That little bungalow you passed on your way up here." She led Gitano into the barn's aisle, and snapped him onto crossties, lengths of webbing that fastened to either side of his halter and the aisle walls to keep him in place for grooming. She handed Kelly a soft brush. "Can you give him a quick going-over while I get his tack?"

"Glad to." Kelly already trusted this horse. She was glad Gitano's mane and tail seemed pretty clean, because brushing them would be a time-consuming job. Both grew especially long and thick on Andalusians, and traditionally they were left as full as possible.

Helga returned with the horse's saddle and bridle. She tossed a square, black saddle pad and then the polished black dressage saddle onto Gitano's back with practiced efficiency. "Want to bridle him?" Helga handed Kelly the well-oiled black bridle.

Kelly undid the crossties, removed Gitano's halter and held the mild snaffle bit in her palm. The freckled gelding took it into his mouth cheerfully. Kelly told herself that here was a horse that liked and trusted people, never having known any abuse.

Helga glanced at the white plastic riding helmet Kelly had retrieved from her Blazer. "You brought your own—good." She tightened the horse's girth one last time. "Off you go, then. Good luck!"

"I may need it. To tell you the truth, Diego acted as if he didn't have a lot of confidence in my potential."

Helga frowned sympathetically. "Oh, I doubt that's the problem. It's my fault. I picked a bad day to schedule your appointment. When I realized it, I should've called you and changed it."

"Why, is he really busy?"

"No…" The older woman hesitated. "I guess there's no harm in telling you. Diego's wife died just a year ago today. I'm sure that's been on his mind. So if he's a little hard on you, don't take it personally."

With that confidence-booster twisting the knot in her stomach even tighter, Kelly led Gitano out into the hot sunshine.

CHAPTER 2

She sighted Diego just outside the barn door. He held Hidalgo, who'd been stripped of his saddle, while a dark, teenaged boy hosed down the stallion. When Diego saw Kelly and Helga pass, he handed the lead rope to the boy and followed them to the outdoor ring.

Kelly knew the next few minutes would make or break her chances. She'd either convince Diego she could do the job—or be unmasked as a total fraud.

She buckled her helmet. It would make her even hotter, but she wasn't about to ride a strange horse without one. She doubted Diego or Helga would even let her.

Mounting from a block, she felt grateful Gitano was not too tall. Most modern dressage riders favored gigantic horses, but being short herself, Kelly always felt more in control on a medium-sized mount. Helga helped shorten the stirrups to fit.

"Any tips for me?" Kelly asked her, quietly.

"Not too many. These horses have a high action, so he may feel a little prancier than what you're used to. You might think he's acting up, but he's not. Once you settle into it, it's perfectly comfortable."

"Thanks."

Entering the ring, Kelly squeezed the horse's sides with her lower legs and let him walk on a loose rein. Her hopes rose when Gitano moved out with a peppy, willing step. She straightened her spine and drew her shoulder blades back until they ached, aware her position had to be just right to make this work. Due to her recent cash-flow problems, she hadn't ridden in two months. She only hoped she hadn't gotten too rusty.

She saw Diego outside the fence near the gate, leaning on the top rail as she'd done while watching him. Under the scrutiny of his dark, penetrating eyes, she felt her muscles tense and tried to relax them. She told herself it was no worse than taking part in a clinic with a particularly demanding guest instructor, or performing a difficult test in a show.

But Kelly couldn't ignore the one, crucial difference. Rarely did even the top prize in a dressage show equal serious money. This time, she was not merely vying for a ribbon or a cup, but for a full-time job. One she needed badly right now.

From beneath her helmet, a drop of perspiration trickled down her forehead.

She heard Diego's inflected baritone ring out in a clear, almost military command. "Collect the walk, please."

Kelly gathered the reins gently, tightened her legs around Gitano's sides and settled her weight firmly on both seat bones. Gitano immediately arched his neck and dropped his head, bringing his hind legs farther beneath him with an extra march to his step. *Bless you!* Kelly thanked him silently. They'd passed the first crucial test. They were working on the bit, the "collected" type of movement that was the foundation of everything.

At Diego's commands, they moved on through a rising trot, then a sitting one. Kelly experimented with subtle shifts in her seat, relaxing her hips, and soon adapted to Gitano's high action. His transitions were so smooth and his obedience so complete that, by the time Diego asked for a canter, Kelly felt totally confident. She no longer even cared if Diego found fault with her position or performance, because she was having fun. God, it felt so good to be riding again! Two months away from it, to a confirmed addict like herself, had been much too long.

As she cantered down the long side of the ring, going great guns, Diego suddenly called out, "Halt!"

It was meant as a test, Kelly knew. She reacted instantly by bracing her back, closing her fingers on the reins and tightening her legs again. Gitano got the message at once, and from his lively, rolling canter, came to a dead stop. Nice and square, head still down, like an equestrian statue. He stayed that way, too, with not even a restless shuffle.

Kelly thought she saw Diego actually crack a smile. But then, he

9

could be laughing at her.

He put her through some more advanced maneuvers, moving sideways and diagonally at both the trot and the canter. Kelly had done the moves before, and on horses less well-trained than Gitano. She mainly had to be careful not to give him the cues too strongly, or he would overreact in his eagerness to please.

After about half an hour, Diego let her take a break to walk again on a loose rein. Kelly suspected he did this more as a favor to the horse than to her. Perspiration coursed down her neck now, dripped from her armpits and matted her shirt between the shoulder blades. The long sleeves had definitely been a mistake, she told herself—it was sleeveless weather today.

She felt the ring start to circle around her like scenery from a merry-go-round, and wondered why Gitano was pirouetting. All at once she found herself clutching handfuls of his thick mane to stay aboard.

She heard a shout, and felt strong arms catch her around the waist. Gitano wasn't going anywhere, she realized.

She was passing out.

"Easy!" Diego was saying, as he lifted her free of the saddle. Kelly managed to get her feet under her as she came down, although her legs quivered like overstretched rubber bands.

"Are you okay?" Helga asked, a little breathless.

Kelly shook her head to clear it. "Yeah, I'm fine. Boy, that was stupid. Just the heat, I guess."

"And you probably didn't have lunch."

"Well, no. It was a long drive out."

"Diego, bring her into the barn, and I'll get her some juice." Helga called to Felipe, telling him to unsaddle and hose down Gitano.

Once Helga had left, Kelly realized Diego still held her very tightly. His arms trembled, and it couldn't have been from the effort—he was a strong guy, and she didn't weigh that much! It must be from emotion, but why? He hardly knew her!

Kelly looked into his face, and saw that beneath his tan he'd gone pale. His long-lashed eyes were wide, and his breathing, which she could feel on her own cheek, was rapid and terrified. Quite a change, she noticed, from his commanding and almost cold attitude toward her up to that point.

She found herself reassuring him. "Please, I'll be fine! I'm just not used to the heat. Office work has made me soft. But I'll adjust, I promise!"

He slackened his tight, desperate embrace, but kept one arm loosely around her waist as he walked her to the barn. "It was my fault. I made you work too hard for too long. You should have told me you were feeling weak."

"To tell the truth, I didn't even notice. I was having a good time! Gitano's a great horse."

Just inside the barn door, she sat on a hay bale and sucked down a cold bottle of orange juice. In just a few minutes, her shakiness disappeared.

Helga took the opportunity to put Diego on the spot. "You see what the poor girl was willing to go through to get this job? Now you have to hire her!"

Diego laughed sheepishly. "I guess I do. Okay, Kelly, you're our new assistant trainer."

He shook her hand, an oddly formal gesture when he'd been clutching her tightly in his arms just a few minutes before. Although that embrace had made her heart beat faster, and possibly jumped-started her back to full consciousness, she knew better than to take it personally. Kelly sensed when Diego had reacted to her fainting spell with such terror, for a split second he had been seeing not her, but someone else. Someone he loved very much.

Kelly didn't need anyone to tell her, after that, how Diego's wife had died. No doubt it had been a riding accident.

*　　　*　　　*

A few hours later, alone in the barn office, Diego began to regret his decision.

He sat at his scarred, gray metal desk and leafed through the latest pile of bills. Feed store, farrier, vet. How was he going to pay them all? For months now, no one had responded to the ads he ran in national magazines for the two stallions offered at stud. At least they had a new foal on the ground, and another due soon, but it would be a while before either could be sold.

Had he made a mistake, hiring that new girl? He'd felt pressured into it by Helga, he supposed. She was the one who'd been badgering him to advertise for an assistant trainer. Helga was a gem, and knew everything about running a stable, so he could trust her with a lot responsibilities that otherwise would have fallen onto his shoulders. She'd stuck with the family through a lot of hard times over the past ten years. Once in a while, though, she tried to take charge of things that were none of her business.

Like hiring that girl today.

Of course, Diego admitted to himself, he also had weakened after Kelly took that fainting spell. She'd worked so hard to earn the job he couldn't send her away. And she did ride well. But even with meals and housing on the property, she would expect to be paid something! His ad had offered a specific (if low) salary, and he couldn't renege on it now.

Where was he going to cut corners? With his employees or his horses? He didn't like to think about depriving either one.

He glanced at the calendar over his desk. Beneath a glorious color shot of a half-crumbling Spanish stone castle hung the grid for the month of May. Most of the squares had slanted, hasty jottings for visits from the hay man, the vet, the farrier, and Diego's meetings with the local ranchers' association, the loan officer at the bank, and so forth.

One date needed no notation. He would never forget it, as much as he wished he could.

Exactly a year ago, he'd lost her.

Sometimes it seemed much longer, sometimes like only a few days. There were still moments when he thought he heard her laughter bubbling from the next room. When he rolled over in bed and put out an arm, expecting to find her there. He sometimes wondered if this was the same kind of pain felt by a man who had lost a limb.

That morning, he'd visited Isabella's grave, which lay next to his father's in a cemetery about five miles from the ranch. Diego had placed a single red rose near Isabella's headstone, said a prayer, and wondered why the ritual did not comfort him. He could not bring himself, for example, to talk to her grave, as someone else might have. He knew Isabella was not really there. The woman he remembered certainly was not inside that box in the ground. She'd gone somewhere else, somewhere he could not follow. At least, not yet.

Diego realized that, depressed as he was, he'd never seriously considered taking his own life. He guessed he must still have too much fight left in him for that.

Right after Isabella's death, he believed he couldn't go on without her. Somehow, though, he had. He'd survived, but no one could say he had thrived.

He'd come close to making a fool of himself this afternoon when Kelly Sheridan had fainted. He saw her slump sideways, and for an instant it had been Isabella falling, and he'd imagined this time he could save her. Odd to imagine that, because he'd never seen Isabella fall; he had not been anywhere nearby.

He blamed himself for that, as he did for a lot of things.

The way he'd overreacted today, Kelly must have thought he was crazy. Then again, he'd had no idea what was wrong with her. It could have been serious—heat stroke, for instance. And the last thing they needed at Rancho Villaneuva was more trouble.

Or more death.

First, his father Bernardo had succumbed, five years ago, to pancreatic cancer. Then Isabella had been killed. Diego missed them terribly for both personal and practical reasons. Without Bernardo to seek out prospective customers and Isabella to handle the office work, the ranch had gone downhill.

Sometimes he almost wondered if the place were under a curse. After all, a rival *had* put a curse on them once, back when his father was alive.

He buried his head in both hands, fingers massaging the black curls to help soothe his overtaxed brain. This ranch had been his father's dream, Isabella's and his own, too…but there was such a thing as knowing when to quit. He thought of the unpleasant American expression, "beating a dead horse." In this country, his Andalusians were still so rare as to be a curiosity in the dressage ring. Maybe they would never be anything more than that. American dressage riders preferred warmbloods, those big hybrids of thoroughbred and draft horse.

Perhaps he was fighting a losing battle, trying to get them to appreciate the beauty and grace of the Spanish horse. Back in Spain, Diego knew, he could still breed and sell his horses successfully. His rich lawyer cousin Franco had even offered him financial help, if Diego ever decided to return home.

About six months ago, the owner of Rio Dorado, the big resort that bordered on his property, had made an offer to buy Rancho Villanueva. Diego had said then that he would never sell, but now he wondered if he'd spoken too soon. That offer would have allowed him to settle up with all his employees, ship his remaining horses back to Spain and start over. Now he'd probably missed his chance.

Diego shook his head. He was almost ready to throw in the towel, as they said here, and yet he'd agreed to take on another employee! He realized then that Kelly never had given him her resumé.

He remembered her saying office work had made her soft, and wondered what that meant. It certainly didn't sound as if she rode or trained horses for a living. Did she have any idea how hard she'd be working on the ranch, schooling several horses a day? And not many of them would be as easy to handle as Gitano! She wasn't very big, so he hoped she was strong.

He told himself he'd been too hasty. He'd never even gotten her resumé, though he supposed that was his own fault for telling her it wasn't important. Diego chided himself for that now. He definitely should have found out more about her qualifications!

He didn't know why, but he had the uncomfortable feeling Kelly Sheridan was hiding something.

CHAPTER 3

When Kelly returned to Rancho Villaneuva the following Friday, with all of her earthly possessions packed into her Chevy Blazer and a mid-sized U-Haul, she found the ranch deserted.

She hadn't expected a brass band welcome, but she could've used some help unloading. *Well, I'd better start getting used to hard physical labor!*

She parked in the gravel driveway of the one-story, stucco, tile-roofed bungalow that would serve as her home for the foreseeable future. She tried the solid, arched front door, but it held fast. *Great!* She couldn't even unpack if the door was locked.

She'd already seen the rough-hewn, Mexican pine furniture inside, and wondered why anyone would bother to lock that up. It looked really well worn, so likely no one in his right mind would steal it. She figured she'd have to get a key from someone, and headed for the main barn to search for Diego or Helga.

Kelly didn't see either of them, but she did spot a man she didn't recognize peering through the bars into one of the empty stalls. The barn was so quiet her step startled him, and he spun around like a cornered animal.

"I'm sorry," Kelly said. She supposed he must be a groom, maybe one of the Martinezes. With a medium, wiry build, straight dark hair, a leathery tan and a trim mustache, he did look somewhat Mexican. He relaxed his stance at her apology, but still said nothing.

Hoping he spoke English, Kelly asked him, "Have you seen either

Helga or Diego?"

"No." His reply sounded cautious. "I don't think they're here."

"I guess not. Rats—I need a key for the bungalow."

She noticed the man wore a denim shirt with lasso embroidery across the yoke, jeans with fancy topstitching, and expensive-looking snakeskin boots. *Flashy, for anyone doing serious stable work.*

The man's gaze roamed over her, meanwhile, with a familiarity Kelly didn't like. "You need to get into the bungalow?"

Kelly introduced herself and explained her situation as a new hire. "I've got all my stuff to unload, and I'd really like to get started."

"Well, let's see if I can't help you!" On the way out of the barn, the stranger offered her his hand. "I'm Eddie Hernandez." He grinned, and beneath the moustache, a gold tooth flashed halfway back on the right side. Kelly placed his age at around forty because of the sun-dried texture of his face and the glimpse of pink scalp through his slicked hair. Up close, his sharp chin and gray eyes told her he must be at least part Anglo.

When they reached the bungalow, Eddie squinted at the door. "I used to have a latch like that. There's a trick to it." He put his shoulder against the door while pulling up on the handle, and it opened with no trouble.

"Oh, terrific!" said Kelly. "I'll have to remember that. Thanks very much."

"Always glad to assist a lovely *señorita.* Can I help you with some of these cartons?"

"You don't need to." She tried to discourage him politely. "I'm sure you have enough of your own work to do around here."

"Around here? Not me! I just stopped by to look at some horses."

"Oh, I'm sorry. I thought you were one of the hands. Even though…I mean, you aren't dressed like one."

Trying to avoid insulting him, Kelly realized she'd inadvertently flattered him—at least he seemed to think so, because he shot her another gold-flecked grin. She felt relieved to learn Eddie wasn't on the payroll.

He explained, "I thought I'd see what Diego had for sale, but I guess he's not around to help me today."

"No…and I'm afraid I'm not authorized to do anything like that. It's funny the place is so quiet. I sure hope they didn't close up shop since last week. That'd be just my luck!"

Eddie's eyes darted to her face sharply. "Is that possible?"

"No, of course not. I'm joking." *He must really want that horse!*

The wiry man hitched his jeans by the belt, a move he must have seen in some old Western. "Well, I'm sorry to leave you to unpack all by yourself, *señorita*, but if there's no one here to do business with me, I have to be going."

"Wait." Kelly retrieved a small spiral notepad and a felt-tipped pen from her chamois leather backpack. "Give me your number and I'll tell Diego to phone you."

Eddie waved a careless hand. "Don't bother. I'll call ahead before I stop by again. *Adios,* Miss Sheridan—and good luck!"

His words were almost gallant, but she thought he gave them a sarcastic spin.

Kelly watched him duck through a fence and cut across one of the weedy, unused fields to leave. Strange. Maybe he lived on one of the other properties nearby.

She was trekking back to the bungalow when a two-horse trailer rumbled up the main drive, pulled by a black Range Rover. Kelly felt relieved when she recognized Diego behind the wheel and Helga in the passenger seat.

She jogged up to greet them. "I wondered where everyone got to. Did you buy another horse?"

Diego laughed at this. "Just got back one that already belongs to us. Well, belongs here anyway."

As they both hopped out of the SUV, Helga explained, "A horse got loose. He belongs to one of our boarders—right now, our only boarder—Mrs. Konrad."

She and Diego opened the rear doors of the trailer, and carefully backed a tall chestnut Thoroughbred down the ramp. He looked sweaty and his eyes still showed a little white from his heady taste of freedom.

"How did he get loose?" Kelly asked.

"His paddock has electric fencing," said Diego. "Somehow it stopped working, and when it does, he can tell!"

"Redwood loves to jump," Helga finished. "If there's nothing to keep him in but a regular fence, he'll go right over it."

Diego shook his head at the big, red gelding. "Someone called to tell me he'd gotten out. I'm not even sure who it was—probably one of our neighbors up the road."

Shutting the van doors, Helga smiled at Kelly. "You thought we bought a new horse? Heck, we can't even sell the ones we've got!"

"That reminds me," Kelly said. "You just missed a potential

customer. He didn't want to leave his number, but he said he'd call again. An Eddie Hernandez?"

Diego shrugged. "Doesn't sound familiar."

"He cut across the field when he left, so I thought he might be a neighbor. Medium height, thin, dark, with a small mustache? Flashy-looking, Western clothes?"

Diego still looked blank. "Guess we'll just have to hope he does call again."

Helga led Redwood off to the security of a stall in the main barn. Meanwhile, an aged blue truck rolled up, driven by a man with a drooping black mustache. The teenaged boy Kelly had seen on her first visit to the ranch hopped off the back.

When they joined the group, Diego introduced them as Alonzo Martinez and his son Felipe.

Alonzo pointed with his thumb at the boy, who looked about sixteen. "I give him a ride home from the bus stop. No one else gonna pick him up, not with that awful rock T-shirt an' that earring!" He tousled Felipe's multi-layered black hair to show he was joking.

The boy responded with a mock glare. "Don't worry. After I get my license, I won't need lifts anymore."

"And about that, I shouldn't worry? Aaiiee!"

Helga sauntered back from the stable, passing the U-Haul. Brightly, she asked Kelly, "All ready to move in? Need a hand?"

Kelly hesitated. She could see both Helga and Diego still looked a bit winded from their afternoon chasing the long-legged Redwood. "It can wait."

"Tell you what," said Diego. "We'll be having supper soon. Why don't you come up to the house to eat, and we'll help you after that."

Helga sent him a sidelong glance. "You have a meeting tonight, remember?"

He slapped his forehead, reprimanding himself. "That's right. Guess I was trying to forget."

"Don' worry," Alonzo told Kelly, as if trying to make his boss feel guilty. "The rest of us, we help you!"

As they all started up the drive to the house, Diego asked him, "Were you able to fix the fence?"

Alonzo's long mustache sagged even further in a confused frown. "The wire, she frayed near one of the posts. Dunno how it happen, but I fix, yeah."

They reached the top of a rise, and Kelly spotted a distant isle of brilliant green in the middle of the desert terrain. A white, U-shaped building radiated parking grids to the north, and amoeba-shaped golf courses to the south. "What's that?" she asked Helga.

"Ah...that splendid oasis is Rio Dorado!"

"Gavin Thorne's new resort? I didn't realize it was so nearby. Or so big."

"About three hundred acres. It's only been there about two years, but I guess he's doing a turn-away business. Gets lots of conventions and golf tournaments. Now he's looking to build time-share condos."

"Ever been over there?"

Helga wrinkled her long, thin nose. "Too rich for my blood. My boyfriend Ted has played golf there once or twice. He runs the Jeep-Eagle dealership out on Route 62, and if they make top sales in the region for the month, they get treated to an outing." She turned to Diego. "You've been over to Rio Dorado, haven't you?"

His answer was terse, and cryptic. "Once."

Kelly marveled at the size of the spread and the unreal perfection of the grounds. "Thorne's got a big ski lodge in Lake Tahoe, too, hasn't he?" When Diego shot her a curious glance, she added, "I worked for a company once that did some business with him."

"Horses?" He sounded skeptical.

"No—public relations." Kelly decided to shut up then, hoping she hadn't already said too much.

Past an ironwood tree spangled with pink flowers, the main house came into view. Privately, Kelly admired the tasteful, traditional Spanish design of white stucco with an authentic tile roof and black iron tracery at the windows. Scarlet bougainvillea blossoms tumbled over a bower near the front entrance. Diego opened the arched door and let Kelly enter ahead of him, while the others followed.

She stepped into a vaulted hallway the same cool shade as the exterior and lined with black-iron wall sconces. The floral rugs scattered over the terracotta-tile floors and the heavily framed still lifes and landscapes on the walls all looked Old World. Through an archway to her right, she glimpsed living room furniture in a more casual Mission style, floor-to-ceiling bookshelves and horsier artworks.

Kelly commented to Helga, "You know, I've seen a lot of Spanish-style architecture since I've come to California, but your buildings are nicer somehow. Better-proportioned and more authentic."

The other woman smiled. "Probably because they were built by a real Spaniard. Diego's father designed this ranch himself ten years ago when the family came here from Seville."

They continued down the hall, following both Diego and the red-hot aromas of chili pepper and cumin. "Nora, I hope you made plenty," he called out, in a cheerful warning. "Our new assistant trainer will be joining us for supper!"

In the kitchen, Kelly made the acquaintance of Nora Martinez, a round woman no taller than herself, whose genial, strong-boned face spoke of Native American blood. She wore her long, silver-shot hair pulled back in a thick braid.

"Nora does the cooking and some of the housework," explained Diego. "Her cousin Alicia comes in once a month to help with the heavier cleaning. Alonzo and Felipe handle most of the other chores."

Felipe told his mother, "Kelly's moving into the bungalow."

The woman's dark eyes widened. "Oh, really?"

"That's right." Because both the boy and his mother appeared so surprised by this, Kelly laughed. "Why? Is it haunted?"

As if on a tape delay, she didn't seem to hear herself make the joke until an instant later. Maybe she felt that way because the Martinezes and Helga all grew quiet. Diego finally broke the silence by excusing himself to go down the hall and wash up for supper.

Kelly wondered if she'd made a clumsy gaffe. What if the bungalow had some association with Diego's late wife?

Nora rescued the moment by responding calmly. "The bungalow ain't been used in a long while. Before you move in, you oughta let me give it a good cleanin'."

"Oh, I'm sure it'll be fine. If it needs a little dusting or sweeping, I can do it. I'd really like to get settled in as soon as possible."

Diego returned, and they sat down in the dining room in high-backed chairs around a long, dark-oak table under a wrought-iron chandelier. Nora set a steaming pot of chili in the center, and they ladled it into handsome earthenware bowls glazed in desert sunset colors.

Diego ladled out a generous helping for himself. To excuse his apparent gluttony, he told the cook, "I really worked up an appetite this afternoon. So did Helga, I'm sure." He explained about Redwood's escape.

"Did he really go over that fence?" Felipe asked, fascinated. "It's gotta be five feet high! That Mrs. Konrad is nuts. She should train him for jumping, not dressage."

"No reason why he shouldn't know both," said Diego.

"That reminds me..." Felipe left his sentence unfinished, but his mischievous grin suggested he was bringing up a familiar subject.

His mother frowned at him. "Felipe, stop bothering Diego. He's too busy to give you jumping lessons."

"But Kelly's going to help train now, right?"

When the boy stared in her direction, Kelly nodded, unsure of what plan she was abetting.

"So," Felipe finished, "that means Diego will have more free time!"

Diego cast a wary eye at Nora. "It's up to your mother."

She poked her fork into her chili with jerky movements, as if the idea made her nervous. "You better not try to ride a horse like you do that dirt bike of yours—tearin' around like a cowboy!"

"Tell you what," Diego said to the boy. "I'll give you three trial jumping lessons. After that, your folks decide if you can keep on. If you do, you can put a couple of your work hours every week towards paying for lessons, okay?"

"Great!" Felipe crowed.

The chili disappeared quickly. After they all had eaten their fill, Nora asked who wanted coffee.

Diego looked at his watch. "I wish I could, but I have that meeting." He pushed back his chair. "Sorry I can't help you move in, Kelly, but you'll be in capable hands. Tomorrow morning I'll help you get oriented."

After he left, she asked Helga, "What kind of meeting?"

"Local ranchers' association. It meets at Sandy's Garrett's place, the Lucky Shot. That's just a couple of miles from here."

"Who's Sandy Garrett?"

Alonzo chuckled as if this were a loaded question.

"Head of the association," said Helga. "She raises and trains Quarter Horses. She's also a crack shot. Every year, she wins prizes in a national Annie Oakley competition. Belongs to the NRA, the whole bit."

"She's hot-looking, too," Felipe added. "I mean for somebody who's, like, thirty."

Nora sniffed. "Don' forget rich. Her daddy leave her money, an' in her divorce, she get even more!"

Kelly whistled. "Sounds like a woman to reckon with. No wonder Diego's afraid to come late to a meeting!"

*   *   *

21

It hadn't occurred to Kelly that anyone helping her move into the bungalow would learn a lot about her habits—maybe too much.

Even Alonzo, a stocky fellow used to ranch work, groaned when he lifted one of her tightly packed cartons out of the U-Haul. "*Dios,* Kelly, what's in here?" He read the label on the side with an incredulous note in his voice. "Books?"

She only nodded. It was just the first of many such cartons, and she was glad none of her assistants asked why a horse trainer would need such a vast library. Maybe they figured she took an intellectual approach to her work.

She tried to grab the laptop computer herself, but Felipe beat her to it. He commented it was nice and light, and after quizzing her about its RAM, speed and storage capacity, remarked that it sounded more powerful than the full-sized computers at his school.

This made even Helga straighten up and give Kelly the hairy eyeball.

"I do some writing on the side," Kelly explained, for everyone's benefit. "Y'know, to help make ends meet."

With three physically fit helpers, she moved her meager possessions into the bungalow in less than two hours. She glanced around at the spare living room with its stucco walls, tile floor, oatmeal-tweed sofa and plain pine tables. A rustic cupboard held a dusty, eighteen-inch-screen TV. An old, red-striped Navaho blanket served as a throw rug and added the only touch of color.

Helga followed her train of thought. "It's not very fancy, or very feminine, is it? But I'm sure you'll find ways of fixing it up."

Noting Alonzo and Felipe had gone back outside, Kelly saw the chance to ask a discreet question. "Tell me, did I put my foot in it, earlier, when I made that joke about the bungalow being haunted?"

Helga replied with a quizzical look.

"Everyone got quiet, and Diego left the room," Kelly reminded her. "Does the bungalow have any connection with what happened to his wife?"

The gray-haired woman frowned. "Not exactly. It's just that the last person to live here was Rico Farley. He was our head groom at the time."

"And?"

"He saddled Isabella's horse for her that day and he used a worn girth. She went riding on the back property, the girth snapped, and she fell into an *arroyo.* Broke her neck."

22

Kelly cringed at the picture. "What happened with Farley?"

"After Diego found out about the girth, he fired Rico, of course. He also told everybody in the ranchers' association what happened, so Rico couldn't get work any place around here." Helga smiled with grim satisfaction. "So if that miserable coyote ever did find another job, it must have been far away!"

*   *   *

Left alone in her new digs for the night, Kelly set up a tall, folding bookcase, one of the few pieces of furniture she'd brought along. She stocked it with volumes on media and communications, horses and riding, and mystery novels. There were still enough left over to fill the built-in shelves that flanked the doorway between the living room and the yellow-tiled kitchen.

She decided she could learn to live with the bungalow's furnishings. They might have been cheap south of the border when the Villanuevas had purchased them a decade ago, but nowadays folks on Rodeo Drive were paying plenty, Kelly knew, for this worm-eaten Mexican stuff! A nice throw over the sofa, some cute curtains in the kitchen, a different bedspread, and it might almost be cozy.

In the bedroom, she opened the louvered doors of the closet and found it ample for the clothes she'd brought. She hung up her jeans and breeches and folded her polo shirts and sweaters on the shelves. Before packing, she'd purged a lot of outfits she did not expect to wear again any time soon, especially the rather sexy, showy clothes she'd bought while she was dating Neal McDaniel. She'd kept a few tailored suits she might need if she ever again saw the chance to shift back into her regular line of work.

She felt guilty over misrepresenting herself to Diego and his staff. They assumed she'd signed up for the long haul. In fact, Kelly hoped this job might be short-lived, just enough to help her through a bad patch.

She'd never foreseen that quitting her last position would have had such far-reaching consequences. She'd ended up with no severance package, no unemployment, lukewarm references and a negative reputation to live down in the industry. She could almost sympathize with the disgraced Rico Farley.

On her dresser, Kelly set out a couple of bottles of cologne, one fresh and light; the other a sultrier scent she'd worn while dating Neal. She added a small, crystal horse head given to her by her father on her eighteenth birthday, six months before he'd told her that he and her mother were divorcing. After all this time, she still felt an ache over that betrayal. She supposed she kept the horse head to remind her of the days when she'd still adored her father, before he'd stumbled so crudely from his pedestal.

Finally, she put out two framed photos. The first showed her mother on her fiftieth birthday, freckled and smiling, her hair just growing back from the first round of chemotherapy. The second shot pictured Kelly herself holding Chacha, the bay mare she'd leased for three years while she still lived in New Jersey. Kelly beamed proudly and Chacha looked alert, ears pricked, a blue ribbon gleaming on her bridle.

I can handle this job! Kelly reassured herself. *Anyway, I probably won't even be here very long. I'll do what I'm being paid to do, and if things get too dicey, I'll split.*

She heard a roaring and sputtering in the driveway outside. Pulling aside the fringed bedroom curtain, she saw Felipe and a couple of his friends doing maneuvers in the road on their dirt bikes. Kelly hoped they wouldn't keep it up too long because she hoped to hit the sack early. Fortunately, the boys quit their game around ten-thirty, just about the time she'd hoped to retire.

Nora had given her some clean cotton sheets, silky with age, to fit the bungalow's double bed. The bumpy look of the mattress discouraged Kelly a little, but she supposed if it turned out to be truly unbearable, she could beg for a replacement.

As she lifted one corner to slip the fitted sheet into place, she found a surprise hidden between the mattress and box spring—a hand-rolled joint.

Compliments of Rico Farley? she guessed. *Maybe that explains how he could've put a worn-out girth on Isabella's saddle.*

She took the thing to the bathroom and flushed it.

Slipping between the sheets and settling in among the jutting springs, Kelly warned herself not to be too hard on the ex-groom. Maybe he'd just needed something to mellow him out so he could sleep on this mattress! Kelly figured that, in her case, pure fatigue would serve well enough.

She drifted off instantly, too exhausted for the moment to even wonder if she'd gotten in over her head.

CHAPTER 4

Kelly thought nothing could possibly wake her that night, but when a car door slammed just outside her half-open window, it jolted her back to consciousness. Her luminous travel clock told her it was two-thirty-five, and she doubted Diego was just arriving home from his meeting. She heard voices talking loudly and urgently outside, then footsteps jogging away.

She peered out her window and read the identification on the cab of the parked white truck—David Newman, D.V.M. Looking beyond it, Kelly saw the big barn door stood wide open, all the lights blazing inside.

She wore knit pajamas almost as sturdy as sweats, so she didn't bother to change. She scuffed her feet into running shoes, threw on a jean jacket and ran out to investigate.

Everyone from the house had gathered in the aisle of the main barn. Diego and Alonzo tried to steady a gray mare Kelly recognized as Esperanza. Her dappled coat had darkened with sweat and she trembled from head to foot. Because the mare's head hung low, Kelly could tell her distress didn't come from anything around her, but some internal problem. The lanky, balding vet stood next to her with a stethoscope, trying to get near enough to use it. Every time he did so, the mare's legs started to buckle dangerously.

Above the worried mutterings of the humans, Kelly heard high-pitched, heartrending squeals. She realized they came from Paco, still shut up in the box stall and crying for his mother.

Suddenly the men nearest the horse jumped back, and Esperanza crashed to her knees. She rolled onto her side with a groan, then fell silent. Kelly couldn't even detect any breathing. The vet pressed the stethoscope to her left side, then shook his head.

Nora let out a sob and Felipe put an arm around her, both of them with tears running down their cheeks. Kelly turned to Helga, who stood next to her. "What happened to Esperanza?"

The older woman's gray eyes also glistened. "Whatever it was, it also happened to three other mares in this row. They were already dead when I found them."

White-faced, Diego told the vet, "I can't believe this! They were all fine when we fed them this afternoon."

"Sounds like we'd better have a look at the feed." Newman stepped into Esperanza's stall, his presence temporarily quieting the foal. "Not much hay left in here—she had a good appetite. Anyone got a flashlight?"

Felipe retrieved one from the nearby office. Taking it, Newman squatted to search the floor of the stall.

Meanwhile, Helga explained to Kelly, "I live upstairs over the barn. About half an hour ago, Paco started squealing. I came down and saw Esperanza was sick, and the other three were already gone. If it hadn't been for the foal, I would've had no idea…"

The vet re-emerged, holding something small, dark and brittle in his fingers. "This could've done it. Unless I miss my guess, it's oleander."

"Oleander?" Kelly echoed. She knew leaves from the pretty evergreen bush were highly toxic to all animals, and would never ordinarily turn up in horse feed.

"I've seen this kind of thing before with cattle that accidentally ate some clippings," Newman said. "The stuff works fast. Causes paralysis, irregular heartbeat, then the heart just stops. An ounce can kill a horse like this." He nodded towards Esperanza. "If you want, Diego, I'll take her back to my office for a necropsy, to be sure."

"Yes…please," Diego stammered. "I can't see how anything like that could happen! We order the best hay, and we've never had any trouble before."

Newman checked the three other stalls, and picked up some more suspicious fragments. "You can be glad the little guy was still nursing, so he didn't eat any. All of your other horses are okay?"

"They seem to be," said Helga.

"I'll look 'em over before I go. Maybe it was just in one or two

26

bales." Newman shook his head, his long, basset-hound face mournful. "Damned shame!"

A grim silence hung over all of them, broken when the orphaned foal again began wailing for his mother.

"Let's put her someplace where he can't see her," the vet suggested to Diego. "Want me to arrange for disposal of the other three?"

"No, thank you. We'll take care of it." Diego sounded as if he could barely choke out the words.

He, Alonzo and Newman dragged Esperanza's body into a vacant stall, out of sight of her fretting foal.

Once the vet had gone, Diego directed his staff to go through the rest of the latest hay shipment, looking for bits of the evergreen leaves. "Wear gloves, and if you touch the stuff, don't put your hands near your mouths!"

Kelly started to help, but he told her, "I've got another job for you. You can feed Paco."

He sent her to the house for condensed milk and corn syrup, and helped her thin it with some water in a bucket. Following his instructions, Kelly dipped her finger in the formula to let the foal "nurse." Gradually, she lowered her finger into the bucket, until the colt started to drink the liquid on his own.

After about fifteen minutes, Diego stopped by the stall again to see how Kelly was doing, and smiled faintly. "Good, that'll hold him until morning. I'll pick up some commercial formula when I go to the feed store. And you can be sure the first place I'm going this morning is the feed store!"

Finally he, Alonzo, Felipe and Helga trooped back from their labors. They'd found the dark clippings in just one other bale.

"Did you notice," Helga asked, "they were all near the outside of the bales? It's almost as if someone just took fistfuls of the leaves and stuck them in there."

Alonzo snorted. "Who would do a thing like that? Don't make no sense."

Diego didn't argue with him. Still dazed, he wandered down the barn aisle one last time. Kelly suspected he was saying a silent good-bye to Duquesa, Contessa and Paloma.

"It's the curse again," he mumbled, chiefly to himself. "I thought that was all in the past, but it's still hanging over us—the Curse of *Don Carlos!*"

*   *   *

They gathered in the kitchen of the main house around the long, trestle table just before dawn. Nora offered to make breakfast, but no one felt much like eating. Mainly, they beat back their fatigue with coffee. There was still one big job to be done before anyone could rest—they had to bury three horses.

Over her second mug of caffeine, Kelly asked Diego what he'd meant about the Curse of *Don* Carlos.

He gave her a tired, rueful smile. "*Don* Carlos was a longtime rival of ours, back when my father was alive. He's got a breeding farm about fifty miles north of here."

"Sounds like a mobster!"

Diego laughed at this. "No, he's the Spanish kind of *Don*—at least, that's what he likes to be called. Anyway, about five years ago, at a big reception after a horse show, he and my father got into a very nasty, public argument. Right there, *Don* Carlos threw a curse on our family and our business."

Kelly stared at her new boss. "Surely you didn't take it seriously!"

Diego shrugged. "Of course not! At least, not at first. But the next month, my father found out he had cancer, and six months later he was dead. Customers he'd brought in, who were personal friends of his, drifted away, and we had to struggle to keep going.

"Then, last year, my wife Isabella was killed in an accident that was just…senseless. I know it sounds superstitious. But the fact is, ever since *Don* Carlos 'cursed' us, this family and this ranch have suffered one disaster after another!"

*   *   *

Around seven, they buried the three mares on the undeveloped acreage known as the back twenty. Diego took the corpses, one by one, in the ranch's rusty blue flatbed truck, while Alonzo followed with a backhoe.

Even Kelly, who never had a chance to work with the mares, sniffled as their elegant bodies were lowered into three freshly dug pits near a grove of twisted mesquite trees. Diego managed a few words about what fine horses they'd been, and how much they'd meant to his family, before he grew too choked up to continue, and motioned to Alonzo to start filling in the graves.

Back at the house, Diego found a phone message from the vet confirming Esperanza had died from eating oleander. He glanced at his watch, remarked that Aiken's Feed opened at eight, and took off in his

Range Rover.

Kelly and Helga finally let Nora talk them into some omelets. While they ate, Kelly tried to find out from Helga how badly the horses' deaths would hurt the ranch. "On a small breeding farm like this," she said, "losing four broodmares has to be a big blow."

"Oh, it will be. Plus, Paloma was pregnant, so her foal died with her."

Trying to be tactful, Kelly pressed further. "I gather the ranch hasn't been doing that well lately, either."

"It's been rough the past few months. Diego's a great trainer, but he's not as savvy about promoting his business. His father and Isabella used to handle those details, and now that they're both gone..." Helga finally caught the drift of Kelly's questions. "You're wondering whether you'll still have a job, right?"

"Well..."

The older woman sighed. "That'll be Diego's decision, I guess. Who knows...after today we may all be looking for work! Something like this could put the ranch right out of business."

*   *   *

Bill Aiken ran one hand through his thinning, gray-blond hair and looked almost as pained as Diego. "Damn, I don't know how that could've happened! I've heard of oleander getting into cattle feed once in a while. But you know how careful I am about my hay. Is Dr. Newman sure that's what it was?"

"He did a necropsy on one of the mares today and confirmed it. But he guessed oleander right away, from the look of the leaves and the horses' symptoms."

The thickset man behind the store's counter shook his head, eyes downcast. "I sure am sorry, Diego."

"Look, your hay has always been top-quality before, so I'm not blaming you. Is it possible somebody stuck a handful of dried clippings in a few bales as a prank? Maybe just before the hay was shipped out?"

"Why the hell would anybody do a thing like that?"

"I don't know—maybe to make trouble for you. Or maybe it was some kids, just being mean. Do you get many hanging around here?"

Bill answered with a crooked smile. "Not many. They'd rather spend their time at a store where they can buy cigarettes and dirty magazines, not horse feed and riding gear."

The bells over the shop's door jangled, making Diego cut off his

29

semi-private conversation. He heard a familiar, lilting voice call out, "Well, look who's here! Small world, isn't it?"

Diego reflected he'd never seen Sandy Garrett when she hadn't looked somehow...dressed up. Even Isabella, who took pride in her appearance, wore grubbies and skipped the makeup when she had nothing on her agenda but working with the horses. But Sandy, although a serious Western rider with ribbons and trophies to prove it, always seemed turned out for an audience.

Lately, Diego had started to wonder if she made an extra effort when she knew she was going to see him. Today, though, they were meeting by chance. Still, her long, blond hair looked set and fluffed with a coy dip to one side that played up her big, blue-green eyes. She wore light makeup, a snug white T-shirt, and tight jeans that fringed at the bottoms over her red cowboy boots.

Sizing up Diego's own wrinkled clothing and rumpled hair, she laid on her Texas drawl more heavily than usual. "If you don't mind my saying so, Diego, you're looking a mite tuckered this morning. Don't tell me you've finally got yourself a wild social life?"

Bill threw her a cautionary glance. "Nothin' that pleasant, Sandy."

She finally noticed neither man was responding to her usual flirtatious approach. "What's wrong, boys? Somebody die?"

"As a matter of fact..." Diego told her about the poisonings at his ranch.

Bill jumped in at the end to defend himself. "I just don't see how anybody could've contaminated that hay without me knowing. I only got one or two guys who help me here at the store, and you can bet I'll talk to 'em. But they're no kids. They been with me for years, an' I pay 'em well. They got no reason to make trouble for me."

Sandy leaned one snugly denimed hip against the counter and faced Diego squarely, drilling him with those aqua eyes. "Only one other possibility, then—somebody tampered with the hay after it got onto your property."

That idea startled him even more. "No...that's impossible! We don't get that many visitors. And the same way Bill believes in his guys, I trust my employees. Helga and the Martinezes? *Dios,* they were up half the night trying to help me save those mares! They all had tears in their eyes when we dug the graves this morning."

"There hasn't been anyone else around your place lately? Anyone acting suspiciously?"

"Well, I hired a girl last week, but..."

30

He practically saw Sandy's antennae go up. "Oh, really?"

"She's our new assistant trainer. But she hasn't really been around much. She was here last Thursday to try out, then she came back yesterday to start work."

"Thursday…was that before or after your hay delivery?"

Diego only had to think for a second. "After. But Sandy, she hardly knows us. And I gave her a job. She'd have no reason to sabotage my business."

"What do you know about her?"

He shrugged. "She's in her twenties, she used to live in New Jersey, and I think she said she studied with Robert Dover."

Sandy hunched her shoulders, throwing in a jiggle for good measure. "Name means nothing to me."

Diego laughed. "That's because you raise Quarter Horses for Western events! Dover is one of the top trainers on the east coast in dressage."

Behind his counter, Bill nodded sharply. "I'll vouch for that."

"I stand corrected." Sandy did a mock curtsey, which didn't go with her sexy gunslinger garb. "So, did your new hire offer any proof she actually did all these things?"

"Well, no…but she said she had a resumé somewhere. And she rode Gitano very well."

"Hmmf! From what I've seen of Gitano, anyone can ride him well." Sandy wagged a perfect coral fingernail at him. "Sounds like you don't know too much about this girl, Diego. I'd watch out for her, if I were you!"

CHAPTER 5

Kelly would have liked to get some sleep, but after the events of the early morning, she was too wired from anxiety and coffee. She showered, dressed in her riding clothes and wandered out to the barn. She wished she could saddle up Gitano and put him through his paces again, under less pressure than during her tryout, but felt she didn't dare without Diego's permission. She supposed she might as well hang out in the barn office and wait for him to return.

The office was a plain, darkly paneled room with a sagging couch upholstered in red-and-brown ombre stripes, and two homely metal desks looked as if they'd been bought second-hand from an office supply outlet. The smaller desk held an older-model computer. On the larger one, Kelly saw a phone with an answering machine, a Rolodex and a large accounts ledger. A calendar hanging just over the desk displayed a crumbling castle at sunset—picturesque, but also ominous.

Along the opposite wall, bookshelves with wrought-iron trim held volumes on horse breeding and training, some in Spanish, and loose-leaf binders that probably catalogued the pedigrees of the ranch's animals. Above the shelves hung several framed photos.

The oldest showed a man who resembled Diego, but with a longer nose and gray at his temples, astride a powerful looking, prancing, white stallion. The rider sported traditional Spanish costume, including *toreador* pants, a black, beaded *bolero* and a flat-crowned, brimmed hat. The horse wore an exotic saddle and bridle trimmed in red, and tassels were braided into his heavy mane. Kelly couldn't tell if the countryside behind them was Spain or California.

Another picture featured Diego at about twenty, holding the lead line of a glossy, dark-brown Andalusian for a portrait shot. A third focused on a beautiful, slender young woman with olive skin, her black hair knotted at the nape, who smiled proudly from atop a dappled silver mare. She rode sidesaddle in an off-the-shoulder white dress with layers of red-trimmed ruffles, and wore a red rose in her hair.

Kelly assumed this must be the late, lamented Isabella. She had to admire the woman's sleek, exotic looks, so different from her own. She couldn't help thinking what an ideal partner this striking brunette must have made for Diego. No wonder he missed her so!

On top of the bookcase lay a few Rancho Villanueva brochures, arranged in a fan shape and coated with dust. Kelly took a closer look at one. She recognized Hidalgo posed on the inside—apparently he and an older stallion, Basilio, were both standing at stud. Kelly was happy to notice one concession to the 21st century—a web site address.

She glanced at the computer and wondered if the site were still active. She flipped a couple of switches and the machine hummed to life.

Someone had taped a password just below the computer screen, suggesting the machine got so little use that the code might be forgotten. Using it, Kelly logged on and connected to the Internet. Information on the ranch turned out to be sparse, and what there was badly needed updating. *That's one area,* she told herself, *where Diego is missing out on an opportunity to improve his business!*

Footsteps stalking down the barn aisle outside gave Kelly little warning before the office door slammed open.

Diego paced in. When he saw her at the computer, he froze, his expression accusing. "What are you doing?"

Kelly supposed it had been pushy of her to use his equipment without asking, and felt chastened. "Sorry. I just thought while I was waiting for you I'd check out the ranch's web presence."

"What?"

She rolled back her chair so he could see the main page on the screen. "Y'know—your web site. I guess you must've put it up a long time ago."

He still eyed her suspiciously. "How did you even get on?"

Kelly pointed to the password. "You really should be more careful. I don't know if you've got any confidential records in here, but anybody coming by the office would be able to look at them, maybe

33

even mess with them."

"Yes," he admitted, through a tight jaw. "I suppose they could."

Because the computer seemed to be such a point of contention, Kelly switched it off and tried to change the subject. "What did your feed supplier have to say about the hay?"

"He can't explain what happened. He thinks someone must have contaminated those bales deliberately, either before they left his store…or, more likely, after they arrived here."

"That's awful! Who would—"

"I have no idea," Diego cut her off sharply. "So, are you ready to go to work?"

"Absolutely." Ignoring her fatigue, Kelly hopped to her feet. "I'm even dressed for it, see?"

"Good. You're going to ride Belleza."

Kelly remembered some vague suggestion on Helga's part that Belleza might not be the easiest creature to deal with, but she told herself a professional trainer wouldn't argue. "Okay. What's she like?"

"She's only four, and she's half-Arab." Diego stabbed Kelly with one his dark looks. "Bring your helmet."

*   *   *

Galloping full-tilt around Diego, the silvery mare made a beautiful picture. Kelly only wished she could enjoy it more. What spoiled it was the knowledge that, before too long, she was going to have to climb on Belleza's back.

Right now that dappled back humped in many a joyous buck. Frequently, all four feet left the ground in exuberance. Belleza always landed gracefully, and the plunges never even seemed to slow her pace. Diego had taken the stirrups off her saddle so they wouldn't bang against her sides and make her even wilder. Her long mane and tail streaming, she circled him on a lunge line. Kelly stood by Diego's side, the best spot in the ring under the circumstances.

Diego, for the moment, seemed to find Belleza's antics entertaining. With a laugh, he said, "Look how she moves! She's like a cat, so agile! She'll be a great dressage horse, if we can just calm her down a little."

"Sounds like a big 'if' to me," Kelly mumbled, under her breath. The fluffy cheese omelet Nora had made her for breakfast stopped digesting and lodged like a stone in Kelly's midsection.

What happened, she wondered, to the concern Diego had shown for her well-being the day she'd fallen off Gitano? He'd panicked when she had a little fainting spell, and now he was putting her on Greased Lightning?

Of course, Diego's reaction during her tryout hadn't been purely concern for her welfare. Kelly realized that now. He'd gotten rattled over her fall because, for a split second, it had reminded him of Isabella.

After he'd worked Belleza for about twenty minutes, sending her in both directions, Diego made her stop. "There," he told Kelly. "She shouldn't give you too much trouble now."

Kelly wished she could feel as confident. True, the mare had worked up a sweat, but she held her head high and pricked her ears towards every interesting sound and movement. Her dark eyes still gleamed with equine mischief.

That's the Arab in her, Kelly reflected. Arabian horses were gorgeous, smart and athletic...but also high-strung. And they didn't tire easily.

Kelly worried this test might finally call her bluff. She'd little experience working with green, or untrained, horses. She might be risking a lot more than the loss of a job, this time. She could break a few bones—or worse.

Still, when she saw the determined line of Diego's mouth, she couldn't bring herself to back down.

While he reattached the stirrups, Kelly buckled on her padded, heavy-plastic riding helmet. He removed the lungeing cavesson from over the bridle, and held the reins while she mounted.

As soon as she pressed her booted calves to the mare's sides, Kelly got the kind of supercharged, jigging walk she'd expected. She glanced towards Diego for advice, but he just smiled, as if eager to see how she would rise to the challenge.

Kelly remembered a technique she'd used whenever Chacha arrived at a show particularly keyed-up, calling working long and low. Instead of trying to collect Belleza, and perhaps getting into a fight with her, Kelly lengthened the reins. At the same time, she encouraged the mare to lower her head and stretch her neck. It seemed to work, and she felt Belleza relax a bit.

When they'd done this successfully at the walk, Kelly asked for a trot. Once more, Belleza started off fast and jittery, but Kelly soon got her moving in a steady rhythm with long, easy strides. She could feel the added bounce as the mare's hind legs began to reach farther under her.

35

"Good…that's good!" Diego coached her from the middle of the ring. "She's calming down. You've got a nice touch with her."

Kelly heard the old truck come rattling down the ranch's main drive before she saw it. On some instinctive level, she braced for the worst…

And it came.

Belleza dove sideways like a car spinning out on an icy road. She bolted across the ring, and Kelly prepared for a buck. She sat back forcefully and chanted "Easy, girl…easy, girl!" At the same time, she saw Diego leap into the horse's path and fling his arms out to each side, shouting, "Who-o-a!"

Between the two of them, they gave Belleza no choice. She practically slid to a stop.

Her heart pounding somewhere up around her ears, Kelly tried to catch her breath. She patted the mare's damp neck because she knew Belleza would read that as a reward for stopping.

Diego took hold of the reins beneath the mare's chin, for good measure, and asked Kelly if she was all right. She assured him she was fine.

"Silly beast," Diego scolded the mare. "That's the blacksmith's truck—it comes here every month!"

Belleza just snorted and shook out her luxuriant mane, as if she thought it was all a terrific game.

Diego studied Kelly so intently she almost squirmed. "Up to then, you handled her very well. And when she bolted, at least you stayed on. Who taught you to ride again? Did you say it was Robert Dover? Or maybe…Carlos Salazar?"

The question took Kelly by surprise. "Huh? You mean that *Don* Carlos you were talking about this morning? I never heard of him, until you mentioned him!"

Diego's smug look told her he didn't believe her. "Then why have you been so mysterious about where you worked before, and your training experience? Why do you say you have a resumé, but so far we've never seen it?"

With a sigh, Kelly vaulted off the horse. She decided it was time to come clean, and maybe that was for the best. "All right, so I exaggerated a little about my credentials. The truth is, I've never trained or even ridden professionally, only as a hobby. For the last six years, I've worked in public relations."

"The office work—I see!"

"Mostly I worked for Fisher & Lyons. They're a big outfit. I don't know if you've heard of them? Anyway, I started out in their New York office, then they transferred me to L.A. About four months ago I quit, under kind of difficult circumstances. I couldn't find another p.r. job out here, and I was running out of cash. I saw your ad in *California Horseman,* and thought I might as well apply."

"So you lied about your qualifications."

She held up an index finger. "No, I didn't. Everything I told you was true. I did compete a lot in dressage, mostly back in New Jersey. I rode a Thoroughbred mare who came off the racetrack and brought her up to second level...but I worked with a trainer. And by the way, I never said I studied with Dover, just that my trainer did."

Interestingly, Diego appeared less angry now she'd explained herself. "So that's what you've been hiding. And that's all?"

"That's all. You thought I had some connection with *Don* Carlos? Why?"

He helped her lead Belleza back to the barn. "Some people I was talking with at the feed store, they asked me if anyone new had been around since the hay shipment came in. I'm sorry to say, the only person I could think of was you."

"Jesus! You thought I poisoned those horses?"

He dodged her eyes, embarrassed. "I didn't want to, of course, but then I thought you might have been hired to do it by someone else. Someone like *Don* Carlos."

"I hope you know better now! I'll give you my damned resumé, and you can call my last boss at Fisher & Lyons. He doesn't like me too much, but he'll at least vouch for the fact I don't kill horses for a living!"

Diego clasped her shoulder to calm her. "I'm sure you don't, Kelly. I'm sorry I ever suspected you. I guess I'm trying so hard to figure out what happened that I'm—how d'you say it?—grabbing at the straws."

As they slid open the big door to the main barn, Kelly remembered doing the same thing the previous afternoon, and an image flashed back into her mind. A wiry man in Western clothes peering into Paloma's stall, and acting startled when he was discovered.

"Diego, you're forgetting something. I'm not the only outsider who was at the ranch yesterday. What about Eddie Hernandez?"

Diego halted in his tracks, so suddenly Belleza bumped her nose on his shoulder. "The guy who asked about buying a horse? But...was he here long enough to tamper with the hay?"

"I have no idea. I found him in the barn when I arrived."

37

"And you said he didn't want to leave a phone number," Diego recalled. "Maybe because he knew I'd recognize it."

"Interesting, too, that your electric fence went on the fritz, giving Redwood a chance to get out and distract you and Helga...at the same exact time as Hernandez showed up!" It excited Kelly to think she might have come up with a valuable clue. "You might want to find out just how tight he is with your friend *Don* Carlos."

CHAPTER 6

After walking Belleza to cool her down, Kelly brought her back into the barn and put her on crossties. She had just started currying the horse when Helga walked in. "Hey, congratulations! I understand she tested you pretty good, but you stuck with her!"

Kelly answered with a tight smile. "It helped that Diego threw himself in front of her. Even Belleza knew better than to run over him."

"Well, you survived your trial by fire. Most of our other horses are easier to deal with, I promise." Helga patted the mare's neck. "In fact, I think Diego could have let you work your way up to this one."

"Oh, he did it on purpose to rattle me. Did you know he suspected me of poisoning the mares?"

Helga's long jaw sagged in horror. "You're kidding! He said that?"

Kelly recounted the conversation she'd had with Diego about her vague credentials. "Boy, when I stretched the truth about my training experience, I never thought I'd be setting myself up for an accusation like that!"

The other woman's eyes softened sadly. "Try to forgive him, Kelly. He's not himself right now. This business with the mares, coming right on the anniversary of Isabella's death...it's making him a little crazy."

"I can see why." A sudden thought made Kelly pause with the oval currycomb in mid-air, and stare at the animal in front of her. "Was Isabella by any chance riding Belleza when she..."

"No. You're close, though. It was Belleza's full sister, Bonita." Seeing Kelly glance around, Helga added, "She's not here anymore.

Right after the accident, Diego sold her to a woman from Arizona."

Kelly understood that. "It would've been hard on him, I guess, to have to look at the horse every day."

"Actually, Bonita was pretty sensible. Otherwise, Isabella wouldn't have ridden her out on the property alone. Isabella really loved her and took her out almost every morning, either with Diego or by herself. It was strange, really…"

"What was?"

"How many things had to go wrong to cause that accident…or, at least, for it to be fatal. First of all, why didn't anyone notice that girth was in such bad shape…not Rico and not Isabella herself? And did the horse spook or did the girth just snap at the wrong moment? I mean, if they hadn't been near the *arroyo*—if Isabella had just fallen on flat ground—she might not even have been badly hurt. It was the tumble down the ravine that killed her."

Feeling pain for everyone involved, Kelly just nodded sympathetically.

Helga continued, "The worst part is she probably didn't die instantly. The doctor said if she'd gotten help right away, she might have pulled through. But of course, no one knew what had happened until the horse came trotting back to the stable, probably an hour later."

Helga stopped herself. "I'm sorry. I don't know why I'm going over all of this with you. You must think we're all still obsessing about the accident!"

"It was only a year ago. I guess it's not surprising that you're all still looking for reasons." After a pause, Kelly added, "Sounds as if Diego and Isabella were very much in love."

"They seemed to be. In some ways they were almost like brother and sister, they were so in tune. Of course, they knew each other as children back in Spain." Helga grabbed a stiff brush and helped by working on Belleza's tail. "I don't think I ever saw Diego even look at another woman.

"Sandy Garrett's been after him for years, even before Isabella died. Now that he's a widower, I guess she's more frustrated than ever! She nagged him to join that ranchers' association, and if he misses a meeting she's on the phone wanting to know why."

Kelly smiled, starting to form a picture of this woman she had yet to meet. "You sound as if you don't like her much."

"Mainly, I don't like her plan. She'd like Diego to 'merge operations' with her. I think he wants his ranch to keep its own identity, and I don't blame him." Helga sniffed. "Still, the way things have been going around here, it would be one way for him to stay in business. Sandy's got enough money to bail him out of all his problems, so maybe I shouldn't put her down. In fact, if I want to keep my job, I should be pushing Diego into her arms!"

*   *   *

For the rest of the day, Kelly handled a few less hazardous tasks. She helped Paco adjust to his new surrogate parent, the patient, old gelding Fantasmo. She also lunged Turi, who was just getting used to wearing a saddle and bridle.

She returned to her bungalow in the late afternoon and sank into a bath too soothe her aching muscles. Her first day on the job, and already Belleza had practically yanked her arms out of their sockets! Afterward, Kelly fell onto the lumpy bed for a half-hour's nap. It helped to make up for some of the sleep she had missed the previous night.

Just before dinner, she phoned her mother in New Jersey. She had gotten used to watching the time difference, and knew a local late afternoon call to her Aunt Meg's would catch her Mom right after supper.

Predictably, Pat Sheridan sounded happy to hear her daughter had finally found work, but disappointed in the job itself. "I didn't realize you were looking for anything like that," she said. "It's a little…below your talents, isn't it?"

"Beggars can't be choosers, Mom. Anyway, it's only temporary, till I can find another p.r. position."

"I wish you'd try Fisher & Lyons again. I'll bet if you apologize and say you're sorry you lost your temper, they'd be glad to take you back."

Just the idea left a sour taste in Kelly's mouth. "I'm not so sure they would, and besides, I don't want to go back. Those accounts they gave me—a chemical company that's polluting sites all over the country, a clothing chain that farms out all its work to sweatshops—next they'd have me promoting Charlie Manson! No, thanks. I'll find some small firm that still has a few principles. I won't make the same money, but I'll still have my self-respect."

She heard her mother sigh. "You may look a long time to find a company like that. And meanwhile, you'll be stuck out on that ranch. What exactly are you doing out there? Taming wild horses?"

A day earlier, Kelly might have hooted at this suggestion—before her experience with Belleza. "Of course not, Mom. The horses have been bred and raised on this ranch. I'm just working with them to improve their training." Kelly thought they were due for a change of topic. "So, how are you getting along?"

"Oh, pretty well. Meg has been nagging me to start driving again. I guess I'll give it a try one of these days."

"That's great. Has your new medication helped at all?"

"I think so. I'm sleeping better, and I think I've been less nervous. Although now I know you're out there breaking horses for a living, I might have a relapse!" She laughed a little.

Kelly knew her mother didn't intend to make her feel guilty, but still wished she could be there to help her through the ordeal. Pat Sheridan had always been calm and resourceful in the past, but undergoing treatment for breast cancer so soon after her divorce had left her badly shaken. Now, even though she had been free of the illness for a good two years, mentally she still battled anxiety and a touch of agoraphobia.

Because Pat now lived with her sister Meg, a registered nurse, Kelly didn't worry too much about her mother's general well-being. Still, every time they spoke on the phone, Kelly started to think, *I should go back to New York, and look for work there.*

Only two things were wrong with that idea. One, she had come to really like California. Two, if she went back east now, she'd have to mooch off both her mother and her aunt until she got back on her own feet. That seemed like a raw deal for everyone concerned.

"I'll be fine, Mom," Kelly promised. "Once I save up the airfare, I'll be home for a visit."

"Maybe you can come for Christmas?"

"If not sooner. I promise."

Kelly hung up without telling her mother about the poisoned hay incident at the ranch. *Mom's imagination tends to run wild these days, anyway. No point in giving her something real to worry about!*

*   *   *

Meanwhile, Diego was making a long-distance phone call of his own. In the office in the main barn, he dug out *Don* Carlos' phone number from his Rolodex and dialed.

The first voice to answer was young and female. When she said she would relay the message, Diego figured her for a maid. He pictured a uniform and everything. He knew *Don* Carlos had a big, lavish home, so it made sense he would have someone answering his phone, and probably his door as well.

The next voice sounded lower and older, but still female. Francesca Salazar, Carlos' wife. Diego remembered meeting her at a party or two. She must be in her sixties now. He wondered if she still dyed her helmet of hair jet black.

Diego introduced himself and politely repeated his request to speak to *Don* Carlos.

"I'm sorry, he's resting. My husband hasn't been well."

"Oh, I'm sorry to hear that. Nothing serious, I hope."

Francesca wasn't about to reveal any embarrassing details. "Just overwork. His doctor says if he takes it easy, he'll be fine."

Diego couldn't resist some skepticism about the overwork explanation. He knew *Don* Carlos liked to live high—good cigars, well-marbled steaks, fine red wines and rich desserts. His expensive sport jackets usually strained a little at the belly. Heart trouble or even diabetes would be more likely. "I wouldn't want to disturb him, then, but perhaps you can tell him I called. I believe he sent someone up here yesterday looking to buy a horse."

This seemed to surprise Francesca. "Really? I didn't know that."

"A fellow named Eddie Hernandez. I wasn't here at the time, but I assume he was sent by *Don* Carlos."

Silence on the line, as if she was searching her memory. "Eddie Hernandez? I never heard that name. Are you sure he was working for my husband?"

This made Diego pause, too. *Don* Carlos might lie, but would his wife? "No, I'm not sure. It was just a guess."

"I don't think we would interested in buying any horses right now. We have several for sale ourselves. I'm afraid you've wasted a call."

That was a little chilly, Diego thought, but he remained gracious. "Not at all. I just hope I haven't taken too much of your time. Please give your husband my best wishes for a speedy recovery."

He meant that, too—as long as *Don* Carlos really did not know Hernandez!

*   *   *

The setting sun painted wide, coppery brush strokes across the turquoise sky that stretched above the desert. Silhouettes of many *cholla* cacti stretched their arms upward in a prayer to the dying light.

Diego sat on a rough pine bench behind the stallion barn and polished his best dressage saddle. The bench also held a portable tape player from which the great classical guitarist Segovia strummed a slow, expressive, melancholy tune.

The tang of the saddle soap, the springy texture of the sea sponge beneath his fingers, and the goal of achieving the perfect shine on the ebony leather filled his senses for the moment. If he concentrated on getting this one thing right, maybe he could temporarily push away regrets about the past and worries about the future.

Was *Don* Carlos really ill, Diego wondered, or had he just been unwilling to come to the phone? Was he afraid if he talked to Diego, he'd say something that would reveal his guilt in poisoning the mares?

Then Diego shook his head, rebuking himself. *Probably* Don *Carlos had nothing to do with the incident. I'm looking for someone to blame. Just like I did with Rico Farley. Sure, the guy was careless, but he didn't cause Isabella's accident. The truth is, if he played a part her death, so did I.*

Diego still cringed at the memory of his argument with Isabella that last morning, just before she'd gone out to ride. She wanted to go back to the doctor for more fertility treatments. They had already gone through the temperature-taking and the hormone injections, which threatened to turn their love life from a pleasure into a chore. They had tried artificial insemination, and the next step would be *in vitro*.

Diego thought, at that stage, they should either accept their childlessness or try to adopt. But he had made the mistake of pointing out to his wife that the procedures also were very expensive, and they couldn't easily afford any more.

Always freer with money than he was, Isabella had accused him of pinching pennies over something vital to her happiness—a child of her own. Before Diego could smooth things over, she had strode out of the house to the barn for her morning ride. He didn't even try to follow because he sensed she wanted to be alone.

But if she hadn't been so angry, she might have checked the girth herself. She might have taken some other precautions, out there, that might have prevented her fall.

Not that there's any point in brooding about all that now, not after all this time. She's gone, and all the guilt in the world can't change that.

The Segovia tape ran out and, in the deep silence that followed, Diego heard a hesitant step behind him. He swiveled to see Kelly standing next to the stallion barn, hands in her jeans pockets and head tilted, as if asking permission to disturb him.

"Hi," she said. "I'm on my way up to dinner. You coming?"

"Soon. I just want to finish this saddle."

Pausing by the open doorway of the stallion barn, Kelly noticed a second saddle perched there on its own rack. She ran her hand over the well-worn, dark gray suede surface, from the high cantle through the valley of the seat and up the pommel, with a slow, savoring stroke. "Wow, what an unusual design! Is this Spanish?"

Her voice still took Diego by surprise. Low and almost throaty, it was the one thing about her that was all woman. "It belonged to my father. He used to ride with the Royal Andalusian School in Jerez."

"I've never heard of that. Is it like the Spanish Riding School in Austria?"

"Very similar, except they wear traditional Spanish costume and, of course, ride Andalusians."

Her gaze turned dreamy. "It must be wonderful to be part of a tradition like that."

In the pause that followed, Diego knew he needed to say something more. "Kelly, I want to apologize again for putting you on Belleza today with so little preparation. It was a mean thing to do, and you could have been hurt. It's just that I came back from the feed store wondering if you could have sabotaged me. Then I found you in the office, on the computer…"

"Oh, my God. And I made that crack about how easy it would be to mess with your files! No wonder you suspected me." She laughed uneasily. "The truth is, I wanted to look at your web site because I'm in p.r. I was curious to see how you were promoting your business."

The simple logic of this made Diego smile. "And what did you think?"

"You sure you want to know?" When he didn't discourage her, Kelly sat down on the bench beside him, her eyes lit with enthusiasm. "Well, the web site is pretty bare bones, and it looks to me like a lot of the information is obsolete."

Diego nodded. "A friend of my father's set up the page for us, and Isabella used to update it as best she could…I don't know much about computers, and Helga knows less."

"I'd be glad to update the site for you. I mean, if you want me to."

Diego grew cautious. "That would be great, but…I'm afraid I can't afford to pay you for that."

"I don't expect you to. I'm thinking of my own job security! A better Web presence could get you more business, at least more requests for stud services for the stallions. Wouldn't that help put this place back in the black?"

"It would be a start," Diego admitted.

He couldn't help studying her curiously. Her simple faith that a little more effort and ingenuity could save the day struck him as so...American. But then, so was everything about her, from her breezy, tousled haircut to her sparkling eyes, her freckles and her dimpled, little-girl grin. He noticed tonight she wore a long-sleeved knit shirt with buttons at the neck, in a soft green, like the top half of a man's winter underwear. On her, it actually looked cute. He told himself not many women could have carried that off so well.

Aloud, he said, "You almost embarrass me, Kelly. You've only been here two days, and you're so determined to keep this place going!"

"Maybe I just think your dream is worth saving." She rested a light hand on his bare forearm, where he'd rolled up his faded, chambray sleeve.

The innocent touch startled Diego because of the tingle it sent through his skin.

"At Fisher & Lyons, I helped a lot of people sell products and ideas that were pretty shallow and stupid. We'd push something as the hot new trend this week, and next week it would be something else. You're trying to preserve a real piece of history—a living art form! I'd be honored, Diego, to help you do that."

He couldn't help but be moved by her speech and chuckled again. "You've sold me, at least! If that's how you promote your clients, I can't imagine why you ever left public relations."

With a wink, she said, "I'll tell you that story some time. But for now, I'm starving!" She sprang up from the bench. "See you at dinner."

Watching her stride up to the main house with a buoyant step, Diego shook his head. He finished buffing the saddle, meanwhile thinking Kelly Sheridan was unlike any other woman he'd ever known.

This morning I thought she was trying to ruin me, and tonight I agreed to let her help promote my business. That means in the last twenty-four hours I've gone from depressed, to paranoid...to certifiably insane!

CHAPTER 7

Over the next few days, both Diego and Helga coached Kelly on her new duties, so she would eventually be able to relieve them of some of their responsibilities.

She learned how to lunge Turi with side reins, teaching him to move in the proper balance for dressage even before he was ridden. She taught Paco to follow her on a lead, stand still when tied and lift his feet to have his hooves cleaned.

Under Diego's watch, Kelly also exercised Basilio, the snowy, elder stallion who'd belonged to Diego's father. Kelly had never before ridden a stallion, and because she'd often heard they were temperamental, she approached the horse with caution. But Bernardo Villanueva had trained his mount well, and Basilio was close to twenty so, on the whole, he behaved far better than Belleza.

In fact, the only other live wire Kelly had to deal with was Redwood, the gelding who'd caused so much excitement by escaping from his paddock. When Kelly tried to teach him the more controlled, collected movements, he often pranced impatiently and fought for his head. She began to wonder if his temperament might be too fiery for dressage, and if, as Felipe had said, Mrs. Konrad might not be better off showing him as a jumper.

But dressage was what the woman wanted Redwood to learn, Kelly reflected, and the checks for both his board and his training provided the ranch with one reliable source of income.

Throughout her daily activities, Kelly tried to ignore her growing fascination with Diego. She knew so few men who took more than a passing interest in horses, or in the type of riding she enjoyed. It delighted her to come across one with not only a master's skill and knowledge, but an obvious love of the animals themselves. Diego's perfectionism drove her a little crazy at times, but he also inspired her—and in more than just a professional sense.

From time to time, whether Kelly was mounted or long-reining a horse, he would need to correct her position by touching her arm, hand or foot. Each time, she felt as if the spot continued to throb with a delicious warmth for a moment afterward. At least once, when she was riding Basilio and Diego adjusted her knee against the saddle flap, he also seemed to become suddenly aware of the intimate nature of his hand on her leg. He'd finished quickly, with a flush to his face. This kind of contact was far from unusual between a trainer and a protégé, and Kelly was well covered up in breeches and boots, so she wondered if he felt what she did, and that's what caused his embarrassment.

*   *   *

During the first week at least, she found evenings quiet at Rancho Villanueva. Unless everyone could agree on a movie to rent, which seldom happened, Diego and his employees dispersed after dinner to do whatever they wanted. On Thursday evening, Kelly called Judy Levine, her best friend from her Fisher & Lyons days.

Judy sounded at least as surprised as Kelly's mother to hear about her new gig. "I'd commiserate with you, Kel, except you sound so cheerful!"

Kelly had to think about that. "I guess I am...now. Things got off to a pretty rocky start." She explained about the poisoned hay, and the fact that, for a while, Diego half-suspected her. "In a way, I can hardly blame him because I told him as little as possible about my work background. I didn't want him to think I wasn't qualified for this job."

Judy barked a laugh. "You, not qualified to work on a ranch! You handled national accounts for us. Compared to that, how hard can it be to deal with horses?"

It was Kelly's turn to howl. "Spoken like someone who's never sat on one! You should've seen the mare Diego put me on the first day." She recounted her adventures with Belleza. "And getting the horse under control is just the beginning. Dressage is complicated, and there's a lot for them to learn. Actually, training a horse is a lot like programming a computer. They have long memories! You'd better do the job right the first time, or the bugs'll keep showing up for years, and everyone who rides that horse will have problems."

Judy whistled. "I admit, I never realized there was so much to it."

"It's a workout, too. I've already lost a couple of pounds, and I swear I'm growing biceps. For a shrimp like me, that's an accomplishment!"

"Hmm...I should pass that information on to Neal. He was in the office the other day, and asked about you."

"Do tell." Kelly sniffed. "Does that mean they've found someone else to put up with his artistic tantrums?"

"Yeah, Tony LoBruno's got his account now. He's already fed up, but at least he doesn't have to worry about Neal trifling with his affections."

A polite way of describing the way he treated me, thought Kelly. She'd take getting dumped by a horse any day.

Judy brought her up to date on more of the gossip at Fisher & Lyons, where things sounded as high-pressure as ever. "I'm so glad you called because I've got a couple of leads for you. Linda Sommers left a couple of weeks ago to start her own company. You might want to give her a call. Want her number?"

Dutifully, Kelly scribbled it down. Linda was a nice enough person, but she specialized in medical and scientific clients. Kelly knew she'd be bored out of her mind dealing with that kind of material day after day.

"I also found a new web site that's great for p.r. jobs..." Judy passed on that information, as well.

Kelly thanked her, but warned, "It might be a while before I can get back on line. My laptop seems to be on the fritz, and I can't let Diego catch me job-hunting on his computer!"

"No, I guess not. Sound like they're keeping you pretty busy, too. Ever get any days off? We should meet for here in the city for lunch."

"I'd love that! I'm off Sundays and Mondays, and I don't mind the drive."

"How far are you from L.A. anyway?"

"About two hours. I'm near Gavin Thorne's place, Rio Dorado. Wally used to have that account, remember?"

"Yeah, right. Well, maybe I should come visit you and we can have lunch at the resort!"

"Ha! If we do, you're buying. No more expense accounts for me. These days, I'm just a poverty-stricken ranch hand."

*   *   *

As she'd promised Diego, Kelly spent much of her spare time at the computer in the barn office, trying to punch up the ranch's web site. Diego gave her what documents he had relating to the show ring accomplishments of the younger animals. Going over these, Kelly confirmed what she'd feared—Diego had hardly shown the horses at all since his wife's death. Well, at least that was only a year, and some had accumulated significant honors up to that point.

Kelly added this new material and scanned in more recent pictures of Hidalgo and his progeny. She removed information about the mares who had died, and a few animals that had been sold, including Bonita. She edited out any old pictures that featured Isabella holding or riding the horses. Even in a couple of the newer photos, Kelly had to choose between cropping Isabella, who held the lead line, or eliminating the shot completely.

Kelly told herself she was doing Diego a favor. He wouldn't want his late wife's image all over the web site, and it probably would have been torture for him to cut her out himself. Deep down, though, Kelly wondered if she weren't symbolically trying to erase Isabella from his heart as well.

She had to admit, she was already growing attracted to Diego. Even at times when they were just sitting around the kitchen or the stable yard, talking with Helga or the Martinezes, Kelly found her herself distracted by his tousled black curls, his deep, dark eyes, even the muscles of his tanned forearms beneath the rolled-up sleeves of his chambray work shirt.

That would be truly stupid of you, Kel, she warned herself. *You've seen how grim he gets whenever anybody mentions his wife's death. Isabella may be gone, but he's still committed to her in his heart. Emotionally, he's still unavailable.*

Kelly reminded herself she didn't need another heartbreak, so soon after her split-up with Neal. True, that had been different—she'd caught Neal cheating on her, then found out it had been going on for months. Still, rejection was rejection, whether the other woman was alive and breathing or just a lovely, brunette ghost.

Kelly intended to protect herself this time. Diego was her boss and that was all. If she felt driven to help him save his ranch, why shouldn't she? She was saving her own job, too.

*   *   *

50

Diego didn't really know what to expect the afternoon Kelly called him and Helga into the barn office. He only knew she looked excited and rather proud of herself, with that now-familiar snap and crackle in her hazel eyes.

"Before I send the info to the webmaster," she told him, "I want you to approve my changes."

Diego had only the vaguest idea of what she was talking about, but obligingly took the half-a-dozen printouts she handed him, prototypes of the upgraded web site. Helga looked, too, over his shoulder.

The first thing Diego noticed was the professional quality of the writing, even stronger than what his father's friend had done for them originally. Kelly had reworded the background text on the Andalusian breed and on Rancho Villanueva itself, to make it more lively and readable. Leafing through the pages, Diego noted she'd gotten all of the horses' bloodlines and awards correct, and described their looks and personalities in glowing terms to make them all sound like champions.

The last thing he observed was that all images of his late wife had disappeared. *Of course,* he told himself. That was part of the updating. He certainly wouldn't want any strangers who might contact him through this site asking about Isabella, thinking she was still alive. Nevertheless, it struck Diego as one more hard blow, one more confirmation that she was really gone and never coming back.

Helga spoke first. "That's some great writing, Kelly. You make the place sound terrific. I'd like to come visit, myself!"

Diego noticed Kelly's eyes fastened on his face. They looked sympathetic, as if she read his mind. "Diego, would you like to add some kind of memorial to Isabella? I could do that easily. A little box on the last page? You could put in whatever you wanted."

He detached from her gaze. He appreciated the offer, but had no idea what he would say, especially in print. "No, that's okay. This is for customers. They don't need to know our personal business. Leave it the way it is."

*   *   *

After Kelly had gotten used to all the foibles of the ranch's other horses, she looked forward to riding Gitano again. He didn't need training, but he still needed exercise, and this became the part of Kelly's job she looked forward to the most. Gitano had such a perfect temperament—lively and alert, yet absolutely calm and obedient—that her hours on him felt more like recreation than work. She hadn't felt so in sync with a mount since giving up her beloved Chacha.

On Gitano, she was able to practice dressage moves more advanced than anything she dared attempt on Belleza or Basilio. And unlike the stallion, Gitano remained patient even if Kelly gave him a slightly awkward cue; he would try hard to figure out what she wanted and to attempt it anyway. Gitano was also the only horse she trusted enough to ride out alone over the back twenty.

She did this one morning after breakfast when she'd been at the ranch about two weeks. She and her mount had to pick their way past low, twisting mesquite bushes; Joshua trees, with their clubby arms and evergreen needles; creosote bushes with their medicine smell; silvery bursage that looked dried and artificial instead of like a living plant; and yellow prickly-poppies that resembled goldenrod crossed with thistles.

At first, Kelly worried a bit over these obstacles, but Gitano proved more than up to the trek. Probably because he'd been bred for similar terrain back in his homeland, he eased past cactus and other thorny stuff like a nimble cat, and kept his footing over the big rocks like a mountain goat. Kelly soon realized she could let him go on a loose rein most of the time, relying on him to find his own way.

She thought of how little chance she'd had to ride in open county like this back in New Jersey, where even wooded trails kept disappearing because of the over-development. It felt like a luxury to ride like this for hours, under a big, cloudless sky, without ever seeing a building or a highway. When she came to a level stretch she nudged Gitano into a canter, and he took off happily. In spite of her English gear, Kelly felt like a cowgirl as they galloped across this rugged countryside with Gitano's long, bronze mane whipping backward in the wind.

By the time they pulled up, they'd reached the edge of a long, rock-strewn gully that resembled a dry riverbed. With a start, Kelly realized it must be the *arroyo,* the spot where Isabella had fallen to her death. She rode to the edge to look down, and cringed at the view—a rugged drop of perhaps twenty feet.

The sun caught something light-colored near the bottom. Kelly found a sloping trail and rode down to investigate. Closer up, the object definitely stood apart from the surrounding rocks, a crumpled shape half-buried in the dirt. She dismounted and tugged it loose. It took her a second to recognize it as a cowboy hat. She punched it back into shape and studied it. A good Stetson, pearl-gray wool with a satin lining, and the remnants of a speckled brown feather still tucked into the slim leather hatband.

Must've been a nice one before it ended up out here, Kelly thought. *Wonder just how long it's been buried. Did it belong to someone at Rancho Villanueva? Could it have belonged to Isabella—was she wearing it the day she died?*

The last notion made Kelly wonder whether or not she should take the hat back to the ranch, where it might stir up more painful memories. But what if it belonged to Diego or one of the Martinezes? The owner just might be glad to have it returned. Maybe it could even be re-blocked. Clutching the battered Stetson, she led Gitano over to an outcropping in the rock wall to mount again.

Only then did Kelly become aware of a distant sputtering that was growing louder. It sounded like Felipe's dirt bike.

Still on foot, she climbed the side of the *arroyo* and peered over. At first she saw nothing. Then the shiny black bike burst with a growl from behind a clump of mesquite trees. Felipe wore a helmet decorated with purple flames, but Kelly recognized him easily as he roared and bounced over the desert terrain. She could see why Nora and the others had made edgy jokes about him learning to jump a horse or drive a car. Felipe handled the bike skillfully, but with all the daredevil attitude typical of a fifteen-year-old boy.

Glad I happened to be down here when he showed up. That much noise and flash might've spooked even Gitano!

Suddenly a chill went through her as if a thundercloud had passed overhead. Standing in the very spot where Isabella had died, Kelly couldn't help making connections.

What if Felipe had done something similar on that May morning, a little more than a year ago? Come tearing up to the *arroyo* exactly the way he had just now, as Isabella rode along the rise?

Kelly could picture it too easily. The bike roaring out from behind the bushes. The dappled mare, a full sister to Belleza, shying violently or even rearing. The defective girth giving way, and Isabella tumbling to her death in the gully.

Would Felipe have seen this? Kelly wondered. *Would he even know he was responsible?*

Did his parents? Could they have covered up for him all this time, letting Diego bear the guilt instead?

It could have happened like that, except for one thing. Helga said they hadn't found Isabella until nearly an hour later when her horse came back. If Felipe had caused or even seen the accident, Kelly found it hard to believe he wouldn't have ridden straight back to the ranch for help. True, he might have been afraid Isabella would tell on him and he would be punished. And being only fourteen at the time, he might have been pretty worried about that.

Or could he have been worried about something bigger? That Diego would be so angry he would fire the whole Martinez family? The young boy just might've seen that as a possibility and wanted to protect his parents. And of course, the longer he kept his secret, the harder it would have been to ever make an honest confession.

The roar of the bike also reminded Kelly of the evening she'd seen Felipe and his friends racing up and down the dirt road between the barns. Just a few hours, she realized, before the mares had been found poisoned. She'd almost forgotten about that, and probably Diego had also.

Felipe's friends—two more visitors on the property that night. Could one of them have planted the oleander leaves, maybe just as a prank, or maybe to get Felipe in trouble? If so, it would be a hard and painful thing to prove!

Kelly watched Felipe zoom off through the *cholla* and Joshua trees, flushing a terrified jackrabbit, still unaware of her presence. When he was far away, she remounted Gitano and headed back to the ranch, still carrying the mashed Stetson.

She asked Helga about the hat first, in case it had belonged to Isabella.

"No, I never saw her wear anything like this. In fact, I never saw a hat like this on anybody who works here. This kind sells for at least a hundred dollars. I know because Ted's admired them a few times. Walking around the lot at his dealership, he likes to wear a hat—he's got a little bald spot, and it gets sunburned—but he said he'd never pay that kind of money. I thought of surprising him with one some Christmas…"

She tried, with little success, to punch the Stetson back into shape, then returned it to Kelly. "Alonzo wears western hats sometimes, but in summer it's a straw one and for winter he's got an old, black felt."

This made Kelly more curious. "If it doesn't belong to anyone here, what would it be doing on this property?"

"Beats me. Must've been somebody else riding through. They're not supposed to, of course, but it happens."

Kelly remembered Eddie Hernandez, the prospective customer who might have been sent by *Don* Carlos, and who'd sported fancy Western duds. But even though he'd left on foot, he'd gone out through the pastures towards the main road, nowhere near the back property or the *arroyo*. At least, not while Kelly had been watching him.

She set it on her own head, and it settled around the bridge of her nose. With a laugh, she concluded, "Must belong to a man."

"Or a woman with a bigger head than yours." Helga tried it on and it fit her a bit better. "Not my style, though."

Kelly took it back from her. "I'll hang it up in the bungalow as a decoration."

There didn't seem to be anything sinister about the lost hat, but she still felt an unexplained need to hang onto it. Just in case its presence at the very spot where Isabella died might not be as coincidental as it seemed.

CHAPTER 8

The sight of the gleaming white Corvette parked in the stable yard set Basilio to prancing and snorting. Although he must have seen a lot of vehicles in his time, Kelly thought he'd probably never set eyes on anything quite like that.

The car alarmed her just as much, especially when she checked the license plate: 35MM.

Neal! How on earth had he found her? She could only think of one way—through Judy. Why hadn't she warned her friend not to say anything to Neal?

Kelly swung off the jittery horse as a precaution, then quieted him. She let him sniff the hood of the big, glossy, white object. "See? It's not a UFO—just a car."

Neal's voice rang out behind her. "Hey, don't let that beast slobber all over my 'Vette. I just washed it!"

Kelly pivoted the horse so she could confront her ex-boyfriend. He grinned widely, as if to show he had been joking.

Neal had changed little in the four months since they had last seen each other. Hair still sun-streaked and self-consciously shaggy, with just a hint of blond beard. In a gesture of shameless self-promotion, he wore a black T-shirt printed with the title of his most successful independent film, *Pomegranate Summer.* Along with his black jeans, it emphasized his slim build and made him look more New York than L.A. His boyish good looks and startling, emerald-green eyes remained unchanged.

Stopping a few feet away, he surveyed Kelly and the horse, and clucked his tongue. "I can't believe it. You actually ran away to be a cowgirl!"

"Hello, Neal."

He laughed. "Is that all you have to say? After I went to all this trouble to track you down?"

"I can't imagine why you did. Anyway, I don't suppose it was much trouble. I figure you talked to Judy, and she let it slip that I was working here."

"Yeah, but she didn't tell me the address. She just said it was a ranch out by the resort, Rio Dorado." He gestured west. "I stopped down there to ask directions, and the only one who knew anything was a gardener. So I did go to some trouble."

"As I said before, I can't imagine why." At that point, Kelly noticed one thing about him that had changed—the lit cigarette tucked between the fingers of his right hand. "You're smoking again?"

He waved the stub in the air for emphasis. "See how I've fallen apart, without you to keep me in line?"

"Keeping you in line was too much work. I've already got one full-time job."

At that point, Basilio snorted loudly and harmlessly, and shook his leonine white mane. Neal actually jumped back a step, and Kelly suppressed a smile. A city boy, Neal had never felt at ease around horses, and seldom came to her shows or even to see her ride.

Still, he tried to show an interest today. "Quite a steed. Never seen one like that before."

"Not many Americans have. He's an Andalusian...a very old Spanish breed. They were bred for war, herding cattle and bullfighting."

Neal glanced around at the civilized riding rings and pastures. "I don't see you doing any of that stuff here."

"Now they're used mostly for pleasure riding, driving and showing. This ranch trains them mainly for dressage. Basilio is one of the two breeding stallions."

Neal grew brave enough to stroke the horse's white, Roman nose. As soon as Basilio tossed his head again, though, Neal jerked his hand back. "Only two are stallions? So all the rest are girls?"

Kelly chuckled. "No, but most of the other males are geldings. You do know what that means, don't you?"

Wincing, he made a scissors motion with two fingers.

"That's right. Keeps them from chasing after every female that comes along. Too bad you can't do that with certain people!" To underscore her sarcasm, she turned sharply and led her mount back towards the stallion barn.

Neal trotted after her. "Very clever, Kel. And okay, maybe I deserve it. But I wouldn't have come all the way out here if I didn't still feel something for you, would I?"

"Maybe you just don't like losing an object from your collection."

"Now, that's hardly fair. You only caught me with Sheila."

Kelly let go another laugh, this one of outrage. "Listen, you just said it yourself! I only caught you with her. I know there were others. After we broke up, stuff got back to me. Friends tell you things, later, that they're afraid to say while you're still together."

They had reached the doorway of the small stallion barn, and Kelly halted. "Neal, I'd rather not even continue this discussion, but if you're going to keep following me, lose the cigarette."

He glanced at the smoking butt as if he'd half forgotten it. "What? It bothers you that much?"

"The hay, you moron. You can't smoke in a barn."

Probably more irritated by her tone than by the inconvenience, he ground out the stub in the dirt. She led Basilio into the aisle and put him on crossties, but couldn't leave Neal behind.

"Look," he said, "I came here to say I'm sorry. I feel bad about what happened...and the way things turned out for you."

The second comment brought Kelly up short. "What do you mean?"

"That you felt you had to quit Fisher & Lyons, and that you couldn't find any other work except...this."

"I didn't quit over you! I'd been taken off your account months before." Outraged by Neal's arrogance, Kelly yanked the saddle a little too roughly from Basilio's sweaty back. "I quit over some stuff involving my new accounts. It had nothing to do with you."

"If you say so. But still—" He fanned his hands to indicate their surroundings. "—what are you doing in a place like this? Cleaning up horse shit..."

She filled a bucket with water and set it next to Basilio. "I don't do much of that. A stableboy cleans the stalls."

"Well, brushing horses and exercising them...whatever. You're a businesswoman, Kelly, and a damn good one. I know you did a great job of promoting my career."

"Lived to regret it, didn't I?"

He crossed to her side of the horse and leaned closer. "They've picked up *Pomegranate Summer* for general release. This fall, it's gonna be in theaters all over the country."

"Really?" Kelly had to admit she was impressed, in a detached sort of way.

"Indie films are hot right now. All the big studios want to be able to say they discovered some new filmmaker. I guess my work caught somebody's attention. And it was your publicity, I'm sure, that made it happen."

She soaked a sponge in the water bucket and started sponging Basilio's back. "I'd like to think so."

"I'm meeting important people now...major industry players. This weekend I'm going to a party at Robert DeFlorio's!"

Kelly knew the name. DeFlorio was a major director. She couldn't help but be impressed, and told Neal sincerely, "Good for you."

"What I'm saying is, I could probably help you get a job, a real one. If you came with me to this party, and mixed with some of these heavy hitters, any stigma you got from quitting Fisher & Lyons would disappear. You'd be marketable again."

"So...dating you again would be a good career move?"

Neal huffed in frustration, as if even he realized how bad that sounded. "Hell, I was just trying to put this in terms I thought you might accept. I miss you, Kel. It was fun having you by my side at these things. The way you'd pick up on all the games those people were playing, and see through all their phony crap."

She paused in her sponging to smile at him again. "Fortunately, I've still got that talent. And I think you just want what you can't have. I also think Sheila must've shafted you pretty good."

Kelly could see by the way his jaw fell open that he didn't have a ready comeback. So she was right—this was just a rebound thing. Secretly, Kelly was flattered he had put himself out to win her back, but not enough to let him stomp all over her heart again.

In the silence that hung between them, she heard someone else clear his throat, back by the stable door. Diego stood there, almost silhouetted in the midday sun. "Excuse me—was someone smoking?"

He noticed the butt, Kelly thought. *Boy, nothing gets past this guy!*

"Guilty." Neal raised his hand like an errant schoolboy.

"I made him put it out," Kelly assured her boss.

Diego ground the stub under the toe of his boot for good measure. He stepped inside and introduced himself to Neal, who reciprocated.

"Neal is an old...acquaintance from my last job," Kelly explained. "He just dropped by to say hello."

"That's nice." Diego smiled wryly. "When I saw that fancy car outside, I thought he might be shopping for a horse."

"Me?" Neal looked startled. "Oh, no! I prefer my horsepower under the hood, thanks."

Diego showed his mild disappointment with a shrug, and turned his attention back to Kelly. "Whenever you're done, Helga can use some help with Turi."

"No problem. Neal was just leaving."

Diego strode out of the stallion barn. Following him, Neal's gaze turned even greener than usual. "Hmm. So that's why you've developed such loyalty to your new job!"

"Don't be ridiculous. Diego's just my boss."

"I'm sure. Is that why you introduced me as an acquaintance? Pretty cold, baby."

She dropped her sponge back into the water bucket with a splash that made Basilio flinch. "Neal, how can I make this any clearer? We...are...over! You hurt me, and I'm not giving you the chance to do it again. As for your big party this weekend, I doubt you'll have to look far for an escort. Hit a club or two, talk up your movie deal, and you'll have aspiring starlets swarming around you in no time."

He acted wounded. "None of them will be you."

"Got that right."

Finally accepting defeat, he headed for the door. "Have it your way. Drop out and do your 'downshifting' thing. You helped me get this far, and I just thought you'd want to share in my success."

"Horseshit, Neal!"

He stopped and stared at her.

"By the door. You almost stepped in it. Wouldn't want to ruin your Nikes."

He stalked off without another word. A minute later, she heard the 'Vette tear out of the yard in a spray of gravel. When she came out of the stable, Helga was still trying to soothe a startled Turi, quivering at the end of his lead line.

"Who on earth was that?" Helga asked Diego, who still stood nearby.

"A friend of Kelly's."

Kelly sensed the polite disapproval from both of them. Quickly, she added, "Ex-friend. I promise you, he won't be back."

CHAPTER 9

The ranch's improved web site drew several new customers.

A Jake MacCallum, with a Quarter Horse ranch in New Mexico, asked about breeding Basilio to one of his mares. He was intrigued by the idea of breeding an Azteca, the official name for an Andalusian/Quarter Horse cross. The owner of an Andalusian farm in Kansas e-mailed about breeding, too, and Diego could legitimately charge him an even higher stud fee, since the offspring would be purebred.

Finally, a teenaged girl who stopped by with her parents fell in love with Turi. Since he wasn't yet old enough to be ridden, they bought the two-year-old and left him at Rancho Villanueva to finish his training, in a doubly lucrative arrangement.

By Saturday afternoon, Diego was in higher spirits than Kelly had ever seen him. He stopped by the main barn's tack room, where she and Helga were cleaning bridles, to spread the news.

"We have to celebrate," he added. "Tonight, I'm taking both of you out to Via Veneto! Helga, call your friend Ted and invite him along, too."

She looked taken aback. "Uh…me? Gee, that's very nice of you, Diego, but…um…Ted and I already have plans."

He cocked his head. "So? If you were going out already, just come with us instead."

"Well, I would, but…we were going to see his mother. She's sick. In the hospital. I mean…visiting hours start at six, and we could be there a while." To Kelly, Helga sounded as if she were making things up as she went along. "Look, why don't you just take Kelly? She did all the work on the web site, so she's the one who really deserves a night out."

Frowning skeptically over Helga's excuse, Diego turned to Kelly. "You don't have any sick relatives to visit, do you?"

She laughed. "None that I know of."

"Fine. I'll make a reservation for seven. That should give you time to get the saddle soap out from under your fingernails." After tossing her a wink, he headed for the barn office.

Kelly felt slightly manipulated. Once Diego had gone out of earshot, she asked Helga, "Does Ted really have a sick mother?"

Helga kept her eyes on the length of rein she was polishing, but a smile tweaked the corners of her mouth. "He does, in fact. And we were planning to drop in on her tonight."

"But not in the hospital."

"I did invent that part."

"Why?"

"Like I said, you're the one who earned the evening out. Diego only asked me along to be polite. The two of you could use a little time away from this place to get to know each other better."

Kelly's jaw sagged. "What's that supposed to mean? Helga, don't go matchmaking on me!"

Helga started on the bridle's other rein. "Well, I can't help noticing you two are getting along better these days. At least he's stopped accusing you of working for *Don* Carlos."

"Yes, we're getting along better, thank God! But that doesn't mean…"

Helga raised her sponge to block Kelly's protest. "I'm sorry. I guess I assumed too much. Obviously, you don't find Diego attractive in…that way."

Kelly felt herself blush. All right, it was hard to imagine any living, breathing, heterosexual woman not being physically attracted to Diego! "It's just that he's still mourning Isabella. You know that as well as I do. He feels he has to honor her memory, and I respect that."

Helga's blue eyes flared, suddenly sharp and savvy. "You mean you're afraid you can't compete with that!" When Kelly started to argue, Helga cut her off. "I'm not blaming you. Of course, it's hard to compete with a memory, an ideal. Isabella had her flaws, like anyone, but now she's dead, all we can remember are her good qualities."

"That's only natural."

Helga nodded. "It is. I just hate to see Diego bury his soul along with her. Isabella was a lovely person, but she isn't coming back. And Diego's a young man. Some day, he's going to have to open his heart to someone else."

Remembering the pain in Diego's eyes when he'd realized Isabella had been purged from the ranch's web site, Kelly found that hard to imagine. "It has been only a year since she died."

Helga sighed. "Yes, it has. Still, I can't help feeling there's something else, besides just the loss, that keeps him so depressed."

Kelly stared at her. "What would that be?"

"Guilt. Misplaced guilt. I think Diego feels if he'd done things differently—been tougher with Farley, gone out with Isabella that morning, or whatever—the accident would never have happened." Helga let out a short, grim laugh. "Sometimes, I almost wish there'd been someone else to blame for Isabella's death, and we could prove it. And say to Diego, 'Here, it was this thing, or this person. It wasn't you!' Then, finally, he might be able to let her go."

*   *   *

Until he stood on the stoop of the bungalow waiting for Kelly to answer his knock, Diego hadn't supposed he might actually be going on a date.

Up to that point, he'd thought of it as merely taking Kelly out to a restaurant, giving her a breather from the ranch and the routine dinners up at the house. But, in that moment on the stoop, the possible added significance struck him. Suddenly he felt nervous as a teenager.

That seemed ridiculous, until he considered that he hadn't dated since his early twenties. And back in Spain, his family and Isabella's had known each other. It was hardly the same as the dating scene here in America.

Once again, he tried denial. *That's not what this is! I am taking Kelly to dinner because of the extra work she did for me. I can't pay her for those hours, so this is a thank-you gesture. That's all!*

She opened the door.

She wore a simple but pretty short-sleeved dress, cream with a pattern of small flowers. Diego had never seen her in anything like that before, never looking so feminine. The skirt reached her calves, but the top fitted closely, with a scoop neck. Light freckles danced from her collarbones downward, towards the merest hint of cleavage.

Her welcoming smile became a giggle, and she nodded towards his attire. "We should've compared notes first. We're both wearing flowers!"

Diego felt abruptly self-conscious about his shirt, a dark, subdued tropical print, which he'd tucked into white, pleated pants. He lifted his arm to show he was bringing along a beige linen jacket. "This will cover it up."

"I wasn't complaining." She glanced up provocatively through her eyelashes. "On you, it looks good."

Because of her long skirt, Diego helped her into the passenger side of the Range Rover. In her usual pants, she could've hopped into the vehicle easily. Just another way, he realized, in which their relationship seemed different this evening.

As they headed down the drive towards the highway, an awkward silence hung between them. Kelly made the first effort to break it. "Is this a favorite restaurant of yours?"

Diego nodded. "It's been here as long as I have. Wonderful food, great atmosphere, and reasonable, too. At least, I hope it's still that way. I haven't been there in...oh, more than a year."

He tried to veer around the point, but he supposed Kelly picked up on it anyway. Not since Isabella's death. For a minute, Diego's mind flooded with images of the times he'd spent at Via Veneto with his wife, as well as his father, celebrating horse show victories. He frowned to himself. Should he have chosen a different restaurant for this evening out?

No. Time to start replacing those memories with new ones!

He felt the silence stretching out again and hunted for a safe topic to fill the void. He found one in the twilight landscape outside his windshield. "Driving along this stretch, I sometimes think I'm back in Spain. The southern part, where we came from, is very much like this—dry, hot and hilly. We even have a lot of the same plants. That's why my father thought this area would be the perfect place for us to raise our horses."

Kelly listened with interest. "Still, it must've taken a lot for him to pull up stakes and move to America."

She's perceptive, Diego thought. "It did take a lot—my mother's death. Afterward, Papa wanted a total change of scene. He'd always been fascinated with America, and he knew of other breeders who moved here and made a good living."

"Like *Don* Carlos?"

"Yes. Even though Papa never liked him, I'm sure that was a factor. I think maybe Papa wanted to give *Don* Carlos some competition and prove we had the better horses."

"Why did *Don* Carlos try to put a curse on your family? Just to eliminate the competition?"

"It was a little more personal than that," Diego explained. "His stallions tend to pass on a couple of genetic flaws—knock knees, for example. A horse like that can be ridden, but it'll never do very well at shows. A lot of times, when he can't sell a horse to a decent owner, he'll ship it down to Mexico to be used for the bullfights. My father thought this was cruel and told him so to his face."

"So that's what they argued about?" Kelly pondered this. "Interesting that your father felt so strongly about not using horses for bullfighting. I mean, as an American and an animal lover, I don't like the sport. But I always thought Spaniards considered it an important part of their culture."

"That's true, especially in our part of Spain. They raise and train fighting bulls on many of the ranches, just as they do the horses. My father wouldn't even go to a public bullfight, but when I was about fourteen, I got curious. I sneaked out to a bull ranch with some friends to watch a training session. And I saw firsthand why my father felt the way he did."

"What happened?"

The highway scenery grew more suburban now with neon signs, strip malls and gas stations crowding in on both sides. Diego barely saw these things anymore, however, reliving his story as he told it. "The *picador*—the rider who tires out the bull for the *matador*—was working with a new horse and a young bull, which was stupid. The rider took one chance too many that day. The bull caught the horse in the belly and ripped him right open. I'd been around horses all my life, but I never heard one scream like that. He kept thrashing, too, until they finally shot him."

When he heard no response from Kelly, he glanced towards the passenger seat. Even in the twilight, she looked pale. He said, "I'm sorry. I didn't mean to upset you."

"I thought in most bullfights today they padded the horses, and took other kinds of precautions."

"Usually they do, but a smart bull can get under the padding. Not all bullrings have such high standards, either. Down in Mexico, there are small ones—the kind *Don* Carlos sells to—where they like to keep things exciting for the spectators. So…that's why my horses dance for a living, instead of fighting bulls." Almost too late, Diego spotted the low, pink-stucco facade of Via Veneto, and swerved into the parking lot just in time. He felt a bit guilty over subjecting Kelly to his grisly recollection. "Now I've probably spoiled your appetite for dinner!"

She chuckled darkly. "I'll be okay. Just don't order me any rare T-bone steaks."

*   *   *

Frank, the small, dapper maitre d', welcomed them with a smile. Although he must have recognized Diego, Frank didn't greet him by name.

I'll bet that's because I'm with Kelly, and he doesn't know who she is—he's trying to be discreet.

Diego took the initiative. "Good evening, Frank. How are you tonight?"

"Fine, *Señor* Villanueva. We haven't seen you here in a long time."

"I know, and I've missed the place. Things have been…busy at the ranch." Diego realized Frank had always seen him in the past with Isabella, and could easily have read or heard about her death. Hoping to clarify things a bit, Diego said, "This is Kelly Sheridan, our new assistant trainer."

Frank half-bowed in continental fashion. Diego wondered, then, if Kelly would be miffed because he'd introduced her in such impersonal terms.

The restaurant's interior walls glowed softly with the same clay-pink color as its exterior. A waiter led Diego and Kelly past a mural of long-limbed figures sipping cappuccino at a Venetian cafe to a table near a tall, potted palm. At least, Diego noted, it wasn't the same table he'd usually shared with Isabella.

They looked over the wine list and agreed on a Cabernet Sauvignon. They spent the next few minutes choosing main dishes, both of them instinctively avoiding anything too beefy or bloody.

Once the waiter had brought the wine and taken their dinner orders, Diego proposed a toast. "To our new assistant trainer, and her efforts to drag Rancho Villanueva into the twenty-first century!"

Kelly laughed. "Well, only your marketing techniques. If your training methods go back to the Middle Ages, that suits me just fine." She clinked her bowl-shaped glass against Diego's. "To Hidalgo and Basilio—may they fulfill their contracts with enthusiasm!"

"Ha. Even if they don't, there's always artificial insemination. I'm just hoping for live, healthy foals."

A few sips of the wine brought more pink into Kelly's cheeks. "This is a nice change. Nora's a great cook, but it is good to eat in a real restaurant again."

"It must be boring for you, out on the ranch all the time, when you're used to Los Angeles. You should get away more in your free time. But then, I don't suppose there's anywhere to go—no place nearby."

"Yeah, I can't afford Rio Dorado, and I'm not really into cowboy bars. Plus, the friends I used to work with are at a distance now. I've been trying to make a lunch date with one girlfriend, but it's such a long drive that it's hard for either of us to find the time."

The waiter set their salads in front of them and left again.

Diego observed, "That Neal fellow managed to get out to see you."

Kelly rolled her eyes. "Mmm-hmm...One of the last people I wanted to see!"

"I thought I noticed some friction there."

"Just to give you an idea...he invited me to a big Hollywood party tonight. He said he could jump start my career again—by introducing me to all the latest movers and shakers—but I turned him down." She sniffed.

Diego whistled. "Sounds as if there's no love lost between you two."

A mixed expression came into her eyes, both ironic and wistful. "Actually, that's exactly what there is between us. Love lost."

Diego had suspected as much. It usually took more than platonic friendship to stir up such strong sentiments. "Did he have anything to do with your quitting your last job?"

"He'd like to think so, but not really." Kelly explained she'd first joined the firm's New York office, then been transferred to the west coast. She went on to tell him about the ideological clashes that had provoked her to quit.

Diego couldn't help admiring her strength of character. He knew she must have made good money at Fisher & Lyons, and he suddenly appreciated what a comedown it must have been to adjust to her current salary. "I'm surprised that, after you couldn't get another job here, you didn't move back east."

Kelly explained her conflicts about doing that, and the reasons why she feared becoming a burden to her mother and aunt.

"Your father is...dead?" Diego asked.

"No, but he might as well be as far as Mom's concerned. They got divorced about seven years ago, right before she found out she was sick. He's a dentist and he married his hygienist, who's about fifteen years younger. They had a new baby right away. He came to visit Mom in the hospital a few times, but... Hey, he's got a whole new life now. That's how he sees it."

Diego heard the unaccustomed bitterness in Kelly's voice, and felt her disillusionment. He knew she suffered not only for herself, but for her mother. "I'm sorry."

Their dinners arrived then, providing a welcome interruption. The trio that usually appeared around eight on Saturday took to the small stage and began playing dance music. Gradually, couples drifted onto the floor.

After pronouncing her shrimp *piccata* "awesome," Kelly slipped back into a more upbeat and businesslike mode. "You know what would really give Rancho Villanueva a shot in the arm? We should hold an open house. I know a horse farm back in Jersey that has one every year, and the publicity is terrific."

Diego wasn't sure he grasped this idea. "You mean, just let anybody in to wander around?"

"No, we'd show them around, of course. But I'm thinking of something more organized, with demonstrations of what the horses can do. It wouldn't take much extra work. You and Helga and I can just do what we do every day, ride the horses—but for an audience. Alonzo and Felipe can groom and tack up."

He still had his doubts. "I don't know. You really think people would come?"

"If we publicize it right. Maybe I can get us a story in the *Sun* beforehand. All we need is a picture of Hidalgo doing one of his high school moves, and I'm sure we'd get a good crowd."

Diego realized even the notion of a successful open house worried him a little. Masses of strangers tramping all over his property? He remembered Felipe had once teased him about being a control freak. Maybe that was true; maybe he would have to unbend a little if he wanted to save his ranch. But still...

"I'll have to think about it," he said.

Patting her lips with the pink cloth napkin, Kelly nodded. "Of course. I don't mean to push it on you. That's just me. At Fisher & Lyons, I coordinated a lot of special events. Once I start putting a project together in my head, I guess I just want to run with it!" Finished with her meal, she paused to appreciate the restaurant trio, which had just launched into a lively cha-cha. "Mmm...even the music is good here."

Diego saw a way to avoid any further discussion of the open house idea. "Would you like to dance?"

Kelly looked genuinely surprised. "Uh...sure!"

He pulled out her chair. "I don't know if you cha-cha..."

"Absolutely. Even had a mare by that name back in Jersey. That's one lost love I still remember fondly."

"You sold her?"

Kelly sighed. "I never owned her. She was a lease. I've never had a horse of my own."

Kelly proved as graceful on the dance floor as she was in the saddle. Watching her move, Diego found himself assessing her the way he would any frisky filly—her high energy, her natural sense of rhythm. He tried in vain to ignore the more human appeal of her body language, even in her demure outfit, as she swayed her hips and rocked her shoulders to the crisp, sexy beat. He envisioned her out at a club with her hip filmmaker boyfriend, doing some trendier dance step, and told himself she would be right at home in such surroundings. Again, he felt sure she would soon grow bored working and living at the ranch.

She seemed to be enjoying herself at the moment, though, and Diego found himself doing the same. Soon they were dancing more closely, matching their steps and trying variations. Once in a while they ended up at cross purposes, laughed about it and got back in sync.

With a final flourish, the cha-cha ended. Too soon, for Diego.

Before they could start back to their table, the trio began a slow number. Diego and Kelly shared a moment of hesitation, then he took her carefully in his arms and they continued dancing. After a minute, he stopped holding her as if she were a rare piece of porcelain and relaxed, allowing her to snuggle closer. The short, golden-red waves at the top of her head tickled his chin, and he savored the innocent sexiness of her spicy perfume. It excited him, more than he'd expected, to be holding a woman other than Isabella, and one so different in almost every way.

The trio glided seamlessly into another moody ballad, one Diego recognized too well. He froze up again.

Their song. His and Isabella's. It seemed almost deliberate, an omen to warn him off.

I can't do this. I just can't. To Kelly, he said, "I'm sorry...can we sit down now?"

"Oh, sure." She looked concerned. "Are you all right?"

"I'll be fine."

After they reached their table, Diego told her why he'd stopped dancing. He decided that was better than letting her think he was ill, or that she'd done something wrong. He added, "You probably think it's ridiculous of me to still be bothered by something like that, after a whole year has passed."

Kelly rested her hand on his and peered deeply into his eyes, but the effect was kind rather than flirtatious. "How could I think that? People don't feel things, or not feel them, according to a timetable. At least you got up and danced. That was a step in the right direction—no pun intended!"

Having admitted to his conflicting emotions, Diego felt he'd broken through some self-imposed vow of silence. On their drive home, he felt freer to talk about his life with Isabella: their decision to come to America with Bernardo, their early days building up their business, and even their foiled hopes for a child. He didn't become maudlin about these things, just related them matter-of-factly, but he felt better for it. Kelly listened so attentively that he finally joked, "Helga once suggested I talk to a therapist. Instead, I'm dumping all this on you. Now you'll really want a raise!"

"I don't mind. I get the feeling you haven't talked about this very much, and if it helps, I'm glad to listen."

Diego still thought it seemed like an awkward way to end their evening out, date or no date. "By now, you're probably wishing you went to that big Hollywood party with your friend Neal."

Kelly scoffed. "I'm sure I've heard more honesty from you in the last twenty minutes than I would've heard in three hours of schmoozing at that party!"

When they made the turn beneath the entrance gate, it was nearly ten. The night sky gave off a faint blue luminescence. Beyond some low trees, about half a mile ahead, a thin column of dark smoke twisted upward.

"Brush fire," guessed Diego aloud. "A little early...we don't usually get those 'til August. I hope it's not too close to the house."

A hundred yards farther along, they could see past the trees to the flames.

"Diego!"

"It's the stallion barn!"

He jammed down the accelerator, and the Range Rover rocketed full tilt up the incline.

CHAPTER 10

They pulled up just outside the small, burning barn and both of them jumped out. The building's double doors stood ajar. The dark smoke that rolled out of the opening had already begun to darken the white stucco outer walls and the red tile roof. An occasional flame lashed out from one of the iron-barred windows, and from inside rang the piercing, near-human screams of the two stallions.

Felipe, meanwhile, tried to fight the blaze alone. His feet bare, as if he'd leaped out of bed and into his jeans, he struggled to drag a big hose from its wall-mounted reel towards the barn doorway. The hose already blasted water and the boy had drenched himself. When he saw Diego, he told him in a tearful voice, "I don't know what happened! I was almost asleep when I heard them screaming, and looked out my window—"

Diego thanked him with a brisk slap on the back, but his eyes never left the open barn door. He whipped off his linen jacket and told Felipe, "Wet this down, *pronto!*"

Though he looked confused, Felipe soaked the jacket. Diego tossed it over his own head and shoulders, and dashed for the barn.

Too late, Kelly realized what he was doing. "Oh, God—no! Diego, come back!"

He threw his body against the big, sliding door to push it wider, and through the gap, she saw more bright, leaping flames. Then Diego vanished inside.

He'll never make it back out, Kelly thought. *Those horses are so panicked, they'll kill him! If the smoke doesn't get him first—*

Nora and Alonzo came running down from the house, still in slippers and with robes over their nightclothes. "I called the fire department," Nora told Kelly. After a glance at the SUV, its doors still hanging open, and asked, "Where's Diego?"

"In there." Feeling stunned and helpless, Kelly nodded towards the barn.

She saw the others shared her emotions. The four of them could only stare at the doorway of the barn, now completely filled with rolling, black smoke. Kelly wondered how Diego could inhale that stuff for more than a few minutes without scorching his lungs. If he didn't come out soon, someone else would have to go in after him.

All at once, a phantom white horse plunged through the dark haze at the doorway. Basilio, wearing a halter and trailing a lead line, galloped out into the stable yard. Wild-eyed and snorting, he dodged Alonzo's clumsy attempts to catch him.

"Here, Dad, let me." Felipe handed his father the hose. Faster on his feet and more used to handling the stallion, he soon grabbed Basilio's lead and put him in a nearby paddock.

Kelly crept as close as she dared to the barn door, the heavy smoke beginning to choke her even from there. "Diego!" she called, straining her throat. "Get out of there, before—"

More ragged hoofbeats warned her to stand clear, just before Hidalgo sprang through the opening. A fringe of flame trailed from his flowing mane, but Diego still held his lead rope.

"Alonzo, the hose—!" Diego yelled, his voice raw.

Felipe's father aimed the burst of water briefly at the stallion's neck. He doused the burning mane, but unfortunately startled the high-strung animal even more. Hidalgo rear sharply, flinging Diego to the ground, and bolted free.

Trying to get to Diego, Kelly found herself face-to-face with the charging stallion. Remembering how Diego had stopped Belleza, Kelly threw her arms wide and shouted, "Whoa!" For a second, she thought Hidalgo might run right over her anyway. At the last minute, his good sense won out, though, and he swerved back towards the stable yard.

Kelly finally reached Diego. She found him sitting up but still coughing hard, one arm wrapped around his midriff. Between coughs, he managed to scold her. "What were you doing, jumping in front of him like that? He could've trampled you!"

Kelly read his irritation as concern for her safety, and smiled. "It worked when you did it with Belleza."

"That was different. You had no business taking a chance like that!" He couldn't harangue her any more, though, because he was coughing too hard.

"Take it easy. You need to catch your breath." She noticed he still kept one arm wrapped around his body. "What's wrong? Did he kick you?"

"Nicked me with his front foot when he reared. I'll be okay." But when Diego stood up, in spite of himself, he caught his breath and gritted his teeth.

There was the sound of more running feet, human this time. Helga dashed up with Ted trailing her. Like Kelly and Diego, Helga and Ted both looked dressed for an evening out. The short run up the hill from the main barn had left pudgy Ted breathless.

"Diego, what can we do?" Helga asked.

"Ted, put the spare hose on the other spigot and help Alonzo. Helga, you can try to catch this damn horse before the trucks get here!" With his good hand, he gestured towards Hidalgo, who still trotted nervously around the yard.

Helga told Ted where to find the hose, then jogged across the yard and opened the gate to another paddock. While Diego helped Felipe with the first hose, Helga and Kelly chased Hidalgo into the enclosure.

They did this not a moment too soon because, just then, two fire trucks came howling up the road. They spooked both horses all over again, but to the humans, they were a welcome sight.

Diego finally sat down on a rock just outside Hidalgo's paddock and, along with the rest of his staff, let the firefighters do their job. Only then did anyone stop to wonder how the blaze had started.

"We don't store hay in the stallion barn, so it couldn't have been combustion," said Helga. "It doesn't make sense!"

"The wiring, she's all insulated," said Alonzo. "And nobody around here even smoke. Not since Rico Farley go."

Nora pulled Felipe aside, but Kelly heard her hiss to him, "You wasn't sneakin' cigarettes back there, was you?"

"No! An' even if I wanted to smoke, I'd know better than to do it near the barn."

Kelly noticed Diego said nothing, just stared at the damaged barn and brooded. His white slacks were thoroughly spattered with mud; his linen jacket, slung over the nearest fencepost, was blackened with smoke, saturated with water and probably ruined. But Kelly doubted he gave a thought to either of those things. She knew he was dwelling on the fact that he'd nearly lost his two most valuable horses, and now had to find money to repair the stallion barn.

She knew he also must be wondering what had caused the fire, and she worried he might have a suspect in mind the others hadn't thought of.

But she'd made Neal put out his cigarette before he followed her into the barn, and he hadn't lit up another while they were inside! *Besides, if he'd dropped a lit match or a smoldering butt on Thursday afternoon, it wouldn't have taken until Saturday night to set the barn on fire, would it? Unless, for some reason, he'd come back...*

Kelly stood just behind Diego and ached to put a hand on his shoulder to comfort him. Suddenly, though, she was afraid to. He might jerk around and tell her the fire was all her fault. That if her stupid ex-boyfriend hadn't come looking for her, and gotten careless with his smoking, this never would have happened.

After another half-hour, the professionals seem to have the blaze under control, and men in long, yellow, rubber slickers hosed down the ashes. Their captain, a fellow of about fifty with a bulbous nose and bushy gray eyebrows, emerged from the dank blackness of the barn with something small in his hand. He gestured for Diego to come towards the truck, and Kelly followed at a distance.

"I don't wanna make trouble for anybody," he said, "but I found this in the hay in the last stall."

He handed the object to Diego. In the glare from the fire truck's headlights, Kelly saw it was a matchbook. Most of it had burned away, leaving just part of the violet-blue cover, with the letters "Twi" embossed in black. They looked like part of a longer word.

Helga and Ted crowded around, too. Helga wondered aloud, "Where did that come from?"

Ted studied the fragment and pointed to the partial word. "Could be the Twilight Lounge. That's a swanky bar over at Rio Dorado."

Diego dragged one hand back through his thick, wavy hair in frustration. "Some guest from the resort was smoking in my barn?"

"You don't have to be a guest to use the bar there. They get people who come by just for the day to golf, or even just to have a drink and talk business."

"So anybody at all could have picked up these matches at the Twilight Lounge?" Helga asked.

"I guess so," Ted admitted. "At least, anybody with eight dollars for a margarita! Wish I could be more helpful."

The fire chief's thick brows lowered like smoke clouds over his keen eyes. "Just to be on the safe side, folks, I'll give a holler to the arson inspector. He probably won't get out here before morning, but meanwhile, don't touch anything." When the chief left, he took the matchbook with him.

Diego watched the trucks pull away with a defeated expression. "Great. With my luck, they'll think I torched the barn myself to collect on the insurance. As if I'd try to kill my own horses!"

Kelly sagged under a fresh wave of guilt. She remembered Neal saying he'd stopped at Rio Dorado to ask directions. What if he'd gone into the bar to ask the bartender, spotted the matchbooks and grabbed some? She hadn't seen him use the matches to light his cigarette, but he still could have had them on him when he came to the ranch.

The evidence seemed so overwhelming Kelly felt she should apologize. As Diego passed her on his way back to the house, she touched his arm lightly and said his name.

If he felt her hand, he gave no sign of it. He slung his soaking linen jacket over his shoulder and stalked up the road.

Helga must have seen the shock and hurt in Kelly's face, and told her, "He's just upset."

"If you think it would help," Ted offered, "I could go over to the Twilight Lounge and ask some questions."

"Don't bother," Kelly told him. "I'll do it."

*   *   *

In spite of her exhaustion and the late hour at which she finally got to bed, Kelly tossed all night. It wasn't entirely because of the assertive springs in her mattress, or even the trauma of the fire.

She couldn't believe an evening that had started out to well had ended so disastrously. Over dinner, she'd felt she and Diego were finally growing closer, and when they danced, she couldn't deny the chemistry between them. She remembered how wonderful she'd felt in his arms, protected and excited at the same time. But then he'd pulled away, still haunted by the specter of Isabella.

That obstacle, Kelly thought she could eventually overcome. Now, though, a bigger one had resurfaced.

At first, she'd worried Diego might blame her for the barn fire indirectly. But what if he'd gone back to thinking she was trying to sabotage him? She realized that was a definite possibility. It would have been clever of her, wouldn't it, to stage an argument with her ex-boyfriend, then go out to dinner with Diego while Neal sneaked back and set fire to the barn?

As for their motive, maybe they were both working for *Don* Carlos! Or some other enemy.

Kelly wondered again what really had happened. Could Neal have come back to Rancho Villanueva on Saturday while she and Diego were out? He was supposed to go to that big party, but what if he'd decided to skip it? To come back to the ranch would certainly have been out of his way, and it would have been a crazy thing to do.

Even crazier if he'd set the fire on purpose, to get even with Kelly for turning him down. He had been pretty mad when he drove off. And who else could've dropped those matches?

She had to find out if they really came from the Twilight Lounge, and if Neal had picked them up there. She sincerely hoped not.

If Neal had started the fire, either accidentally or on purpose, Diego probably would never trust her again.

*   *   *

The arson investigator came out the next morning to check the barn and surrounding property. He admitted to them later he found no accelerant such as gasoline, and nothing to identify the culprit. The scrap of matchbook had been too soggy to yield any fingerprints. The tire tracks in the main barnyard all came from familiar vehicles, including Neal's car. The ground near the stallion barn had gotten too messed up with water from the hoses, and prints from the people and horses, to provide any helpful information.

Diego didn't show up at breakfast. When Kelly asked, Helga said he'd gone to the doctor to have the pain in his side checked out, at her insistence.

"I think he's got a cracked rib," she said. "He put up a fuss, but he went."

"That's good." Kelly took a swallow of her coffee before she added, "I thought he might still be avoiding me."

"Don't be silly. Why would he do that?"

Kelly pointed out the reasons why the fire might have revived his suspicions about her, and Helga tried to dismiss the notion. "It wasn't even your idea to go out Saturday. It was his. He might as well suspect me. After all, I insisted on staying behind with Ted!"

"Ah, but he's known you for ten years, and me for only about a month. A pretty scary month."

Helga wouldn't accept this. "You risked your neck to help us last night, Kelly. I really don't think he has any doubts about your loyalties."

"Maybe not. Just in case, though, I have to find out what really happened, and if Neal could've been involved. Can you spare me for an hour or so? I want to drop over to Rio Dorado."

*   *   *

As she crossed onto the resort property, the landscape magically transformed from brown and rocky to green and carpet-smooth. State-of-the-art irrigation and fertilization made Rio Dorado a lush oasis in the midst of the near-desert terrain.

Kelly parked her Blazer between a Mercedes and a Lexus, and headed for the glassy front entrance. She passed prosperous-looking folks who emerged from white Rio Dorado limousines and tipped uniformed bellmen to load their bags onto gleaming brass carts. She felt obliged to use the doormats—monogrammed with an overlapping, gilded R and D—to wipe off the dirt and whatever else might be clinging to her paddock boots, before she stepped inside.

In the lobby, she crossed a marble floor polished to mirror brightness, flanked by towering, potted palms. While the arriving guests bustled past her to the front desk, Kelly scanned for directional signs. Elevators and conference rooms to the left, restaurants to the right. She followed the arrows marked RESTAURANTS, the closest thing to what she was looking for.

She passed a sunny, Southwestern-style café that served breakfast and lunch, and a more elegant, dusky room offering only dinner. Past these, en route to the pool, she came upon the Twilight Lounge.

Even before Kelly stepped through the door, she knew she was in the right place. The carpeting, the printed upholstery of the booths, and even the strip lighting over the bar all echoed the same violet-blue shade as the matchbook cover. If she still had any doubts, a bowl at the cashier's stand held about two dozen more of the matchbooks.

Well, I know where it came from, she told herself. *Now I just have to find out if Neal was the one who dropped it in that empty stall.*

She sat down at the bar. Normally, she'd have felt conspicuous perching on a barstool, unescorted, in the middle of the day. But because this place was so pricey, it took on an air of respectability. Men and women in well-pressed shorts and tops, some looking fresh from the golf course, sipped Bloody Marys and gin-and-tonics. The only person who seemed serious about getting plastered was a thin, dark-skinned guy with straight black hair gathered in a tail down his back. His long, chiseled face impressed Kelly as Native American.

After her initial glance around, she caught the eye of the rosy-cheeked, collegiate-looking bartender. "Excuse me—were you working here yesterday?"

When he nodded, Kelly asked him if he'd seen anyone fitting Neal's description. She added, "He had on a weird T-shirt—it said *Pomegranate Summer* on the front."

The bartender frowned doubtfully. "Don't remember anyone like that. I start at noon, though. If he came in earlier, I wouldn't know."

He probably had, thought Kelly. Neal had shown up at the stable around eleven. And even if no one remembered seeing him, he still could have grabbed a few books of matches from the bowl near the cash register.

While she considered her next move, she grew aware of a disturbance a few bar stools away. She guessed, even before she looked, that it involved the guy with the long, black ponytail. He was arguing with a tall man in crisp khakis and a white polo shirt whose silver temples glinted against his rich tan.

The taller man bent over the long-haired guy with an air of authority, laying down the law, while the other fellow hunched over his drink in a sullen way. Kelly couldn't hear their conversation; just Silver Temples whispering in a series of whip cracks and Ponytail muttering in reply.

"What's all that about?"

To her surprised, the bartender actually had an answer. "Oh, Thorne's reaming out his chopper guy again."

Since the two men wouldn't notice her, anyway, Kelly felt free to stare. So that was Gavin Thorne, himself. "Chopper...you mean, helicopter?"

The bartender nodded. "There's a helipad on top of the resort. Thorne uses it to get to the airport, take special visitors around, and stuff like that. Sometimes he goes out on short notice, so I guess I can see why he wouldn't want Joe getting crocked in the middle of the day."

Kelly watched Thorne and his pilot, still engaged in a hushed but intense argument. "I'm amazed the guy keeps his job."

"It's a shame really. Joe's an okay guy, and he never used to drink like this. Only got bad the last year or so." Hailed then by a woman in a brightly flowered sundress, the young, talkative bartender went back to work.

On her way out through the lobby, Kelly spotted brochures for the resort on a glass-topped, bamboo table, and stuffed one into her backpack. At least she'd finally had a look around Rio Dorado.

Unfortunately, she still hadn't gotten what she needed. Proof of Neal's innocence—and, by association, her own.

CHAPTER 11

Even though she had never expected to use it again, Kelly still had Neal's home phone number in her address book. Truth be told, she still knew it by heart. After she returned from Rio Dorado, she knew she had to make the call, in hopes of getting a straight answer. She used the phone in the yellow kitchen of her bungalow to be sure of privacy.

A woman answered. In a babyish-sounding voice, she told Neal, "It's for you."

Well, wouldn't it be? Kelly mocked her silently. *It's his apartment! Are you really as dumb as you sound?*

Of course, maybe you and he have been living together for a while, so you've made yourself at home by now. But if that were the case, I doubt he would've come out to the ranch last week looking for me!

When Neal heard Kelly on the line, he went into full gloating mode. "Hah! Having second thoughts about turning me down? It's a little late for that now. I told you you'd be sorry!"

Kelly reeled with fury. He actually had set the fire. And deliberately, to make her "sorry." "Neal, I can't believe this! I always knew you were impulsive, but I never dreamed you could do anything so despicable, so cruel—"

"Oh, please. What did you expect me to do, nothing? After the way you blew me off? And after your Latin-heartthrob boss looked down his nose at me, just because I littered up his barnyard with one stupid cigarette butt? I had to find some way to salve my wounds, didn't I?"

He's talking like a real psycho! Kelly thought. It scared her to think

80

she had misjudged his character so badly. "I ought to turn you in to the cops, but I don't suppose they'd ever be able to link the matchbook to you. You're just lucky both horses are okay, and the barn can be salvaged. I don't know if I can say the same about my job—"

He cut her off. "Hey, whoa! What the hell are you talking about?"

"What do you think? The fire, of course."

"What fire?"

"The one you set in the stallion barn on Saturday. We found part of the matchbook from Rio Dorado."

She heard silence, which could mean Neal was either making up an alibi or was genuinely surprised. "You've got to be kidding. Why would I do a thing like that?"

"Because you were mad at me."

He laughed darkly. "Sure, Kel, I was mad when I left, but I got over it. I went to that party in Malibu on Saturday, remember? I don't know when this fire started, but I got to the party around seven. Wanna know who I talked to?" He reeled off a few stellar names. "Sounds like I'd have had to cover a lot of miles to get to your ranch and back out to the coast!"

He could've come by earlier in the day, Kelly thought, *but then somebody probably would have seen him.* Between four and six, Diego and the rest of them had still been milling around the barns, feeding the horses and finishing up chores. And how long could a cigarette smolder in a pile of dry hay? "If you didn't start the fire, what did you mean about making me sorry and getting even—all that stuff you said before?"

"I was talking about Lacey, the lovely, young thing who answered the phone. I met her at the party, and we've been inseparable ever since. I thought that's what you were so ticked off about."

Kelly sighed. She couldn't be bothered with either embarrassment or jealousy, because she felt so relieved. "God, sleep with anybody you want to. I already know you're a tomcat. I'm just glad to hear you're not an arsonist."

"You honestly thought I was?"

"I didn't want to. But you were hanging around that barn with me on Thursday, and you said you'd been out to Rio Dorado. No one here smokes, so I didn't know who else to blame."

"Well, you'd better keep looking. If it's not one of the staff, it's gotta be one of the horses." A pause, and a shift to greater seriousness. "Kel, you're all right, aren't you? You weren't hurt?"

"I'm fine. Thanks for asking—better late than never."

"Hey, you were hammering me so hard, I never had the chance." She heard the woman's sugary voice again, coaxing him away from the phone. "I gotta go…Look, I'm sorry you had a problem, and I hope you get it fixed real soon, okay?"

"Thanks, Neal. Have a nice life."

Hanging up, Kelly finally let herself feel some bitterness at the fact he had gotten over her so quickly. But she didn't dwell for long on that idea because another, more pressing one demanded her attention.

If Neal had started the fire, at least she would have know his motive—simply jealousy—and could be pretty sure he wouldn't strike again. If she knew nothing about the arsonist, though, he could still be out there somewhere, frustrated because he hadn't accomplished his goal.

And that meant he could still be dangerous.

*   *   *

Kelly found Diego near the stallion barn, saying goodbye to a paunchy man in a jacket and tie, who drove off in a late-model black sedan. Before she could ask, Diego explained to her, "Insurance adjuster."

"You'll be able to collect, I hope?"

"It may not be so easy. This case looks so much like arson, I may have to prove I didn't set the fire myself."

"How are you going to do that?" Kelly asked.

He shrugged. "Only one way I can think of—find the person who did do it."

Kelly saw her opening. "Diego, I hope you're not thinking I had anything to do with this."

His manner remained cool. "How could you have? You had the perfect alibi. You were with me when the place caught fire."

"But Neal could have done it. That's what you've been thinking, isn't it?"

"He is the only person I've seen smoking around the barn."

"I thought of that myself, so I called him. He was at that big party in Malibu on Saturday night. He dropped the names of two or three well-known people I could call—or you could call—to verify his story. If that's true, there's no way Neal could've come by here after we left for the restaurant, and still made it back to the party."

When Diego still appeared to waffle, Kelly held out a scrap of paper. "Want the names he gave me?"

"No," he relented. "But what other explanation is there? How did those matches get in the hay?"

"It could've been someone who came by the ranch out of curiosity, but didn't stay to talk to anyone. It could even have been Felipe—maybe he lied about sneaking cigarettes. But I figure it was probably the same person who contaminated the hay, whoever that may have been."

"That's what I think, too."

She smiled again, more grimly. "Just before I left Fisher & Lyons, I did p.r. for some big corporations. One CEO was a real paranoid guy, and he had a quotation framed on his wall. I think it was from Ian Fleming—you know, the guy who created James Bond?"

Diego nodded. Kelly figured he had to have seen James Bond movies, even in Spain.

"Anyway, it said, 'Once is happenstance, twice is coincidence, three times is enemy action.' I think you do have an enemy. I just want you to know for certain Neal isn't working for him, and neither am I!"

Diego looked embarrassed. "Of course you aren't. I never thought that."

She eyed the clumsy new bulge beneath his knit shirt, just above the waist. "What did the doctor say about your rib?"

He pulled the shirt up to show her a medical brace, fastened with Velcro. "It's cracked, just like Helga said. I guess she learned something from those veterinary courses she took back in Germany. The doctor said I can't ride for six weeks—we'll just see about that! But even for a few weeks, it puts a more work onto you and Helga."

"Speaking of whom..." said Kelly.

Helga came striding up the hill, just then, with a wave. "Diego, you had a call from Ms. Garrett. She's upset because you didn't RSVP to that fundraiser at the country club. She says she went out of her way to get you invited. She wants to make sure you're coming on Friday."

Diego grimaced. "Tell her I've got a cracked rib and a barn to rebuild."

"What fundraiser?" Kelly asked.

"For Steven Brooks, the guy running for the state assembly."

"He's very supportive of open space issues in this district," Helga explained. "Y'know, protecting farms and recreational land from over-development."

Kelly's ears pricked the way Redwood's must have when he spotted a nice, challenging fence to jump. "Diego, if you got an invitation, I think you should go. It sounds like a good chance to promote your business."

"I don't want to leave this place unguarded for another evening!"

"The fundraiser's in the afternoon," Helga reminded him. "Two to five."

"It's also a fifty-dollar ticket."

"Think of it as an investment," Kelly urged him. "Remember, if Brooks gets elected, it means tax breaks for ranchers!"

Helga planted her hands on her hips and studied him as if she were a disapproving aunt. "You're just looking for an excuse because you hate these social things."

"You're right. I do. And I think I'm in enough pain already." He turned to Kelly with an evil glint. "If you think it's such a great idea, come with me."

"Gladly. Two can network better than one. I'll even pay for my own ticket."

He laughed. "No, you won't. I know how much you make!"

"Helga, you'll be left on guard alone," Kelly told her. "Think you can handle it?"

"In the middle of the afternoon, I think so. Do I have time to ask Sandy Garrett for some sharpshooting lessons?"

Kelly told Diego, "You can bring a cell phone, so Helga can reach us quickly if anything does happen."

"Not a bad idea," he admitted. "I'll tell the Martinezes to keep watch, too. It should be safe enough, I guess. After all," he reminded Kelly, "we've only had two occurrences so far. According to your theory, that's still just 'coincidence.'"

*   *   *

Diego contacted an agent from a security firm that came out to the ranch the next day. At dinner, Diego told everyone he was installing smoke alarms in both barns and motion-sensitive lighting in the barnyards. In addition, he was rigging sensors at the barn doors that would alert him up at the house if anyone broke in at night.

"I think we should just get a big, mean dog," said Felipe.

Diego smiled. "We'd have to turn him loose at night. I don't think that would go over well with the barn cats, and we need them to keep mice out of the grain."

"Will they trigger the alarms?" asked Kelly.

"Just the motion lights. The door sensors will only pick up something big, like a person or a horse. The guy tried to sell me on all kinds of things for the house, too, but I don't think that's necessary. Even if someone is trying to ruin me, so far he's only gone after the horses."

At first, Kelly was inclined to agree, but later she had second thoughts.

*   *   *

She was watching TV in the living room of her bungalow, and the white-knuckle mystery plot might have affected her frame of mind. During a commercial, her gaze fell on the battered Western hat she'd hung from a bare nail on the wall.

If it didn't belong to anyone at Rancho Villaneuva, it could represent a third time someone had trespassed on the property. A long time ago, from the look of the hat. And in the same *arroyo* where Isabella had met her death.

Kelly remembered what Helga had said about all the coincidences that had conspired to make Isabella's fall a fatal one. Was it possible her death hadn't been an accident, but part of the same pattern?

If so, Diego was wrong. The saboteur wouldn't stop at harming the horses. He was willing to kill people, as well—maybe he already had!

Kelly decided she wouldn't mention this possibility to Diego, at least not until she had real evidence. It would hurt him too much, and she didn't want to do that without good reason.

Enemy action, she thought, pondering the Stetson. But who was the enemy? A stranger, or someone Diego already knew well?

CHAPTER 12

Diego had to admit, he felt more confident approaching the afternoon fundraiser with Kelly at his side. He wouldn't have done this on his own—driven between the stone pillars of the country club and up the long, private road, to mingle with a bunch of strangers. He kept thinking of the work he was leaving undone at the ranch, then reminded himself he was hampered, anyway, by his taped rib. Right now, he probably wasn't in shape for anything much more strenuous than sipping wine and gabbing with other business and property owners from the area.

He supposed he was like an artist who wanted only to paint, but had no talent for promoting his work. He could think only that his father should be there instead of him. Bernardo Villaneuva always knew what to say to everyone, from the governor down to a five-year-old. Of course, he also felt free to speak his mind on an issue, which was how he'd alienated *Don* Carlos.

Next to his father, Diego had always felt introverted and tongue-tied. But he would have to get over that, he told himself. Maybe with Kelly's help, he could.

Even to Diego, the white-columned country club looked as if it would have been more at home surrounded by magnolia trees in the southeastern U.S. than by date palms in this part of California. A valet took the Range Rover away, and Diego and Kelly climbed the wide front steps.

Kelly the Chameleon had undergone another startling style change today, Diego noticed. For this businesslike occasion, she wore a teal-green suit that looked like silk, short at the hem and nipped at the waist. The jacket neckline dipped well below her collarbone, and she didn't seem to be wearing any blouse underneath.

Diego started to scold himself for even speculating about such a thing, then wondered why. After all, he was a single man again. Yes, but she was also his employee—that still made the situation awkward. Oh well, there was no law against looking! After all, he realized, people here were probably going to assume she'd come as his date.

Just inside the ballroom doorway, a white-haired society matron seated at a card table handed them ID tags that included the name of their business. Diego pinned his to the lapel of his navy blazer. Kelly had some trouble getting through the silky fabric of her jacket, and he tried again not to look as, for a moment, her neckline slipped around precariously.

Patriotic, tricolor bunting festooned the tasteful Georgian ballroom. A mural-sized photo of the blond, boyish, clean-cut candidate hung behind the dais. Just in front of it, Stephen Brooks himself mingled with the guests. Kelly and Diego dropped by to say hello. They thanked Brooks for supporting tax breaks for local ranchers and a bill to preserve the region's open spaces.

Afterward, Kelly whispered to Diego, "There, that wasn't so hard, was it?"

He faked a shudder. "I complimented a politician! What am I turning into?"

A high-pitched but male voice hailed him. "Diego Villanueva, is that you?"

He barely recognized the small man with thick glasses and a red-white-and-blue bow tie, until he read the nametag. Bob Weimer, president of the county historical society. Diego had met him briefly four or five years back when he and Isabella had taken part in a parade. Spanish Heritage Week or something like that.

After Diego introduced Kelly, Weimer explained the connection to her. "Diego probably doesn't remember me because we barely had a chance to talk that day. But I remember what a striking presence he made in the parade. He and his wife, both in traditional Spanish costumes, on two beautiful gray horses. All that excitement, and the horses were so well behaved!"

Diego found himself recalling the day fondly as well. He hadn't thought about it in a long time. "It was very kind of you to invite us to take part."

"Seemed only logical, since your ranch is one of the few pieces of authentic Spanish heritage we have in this county." Lowering his voice, Weimer added, "I was terribly sorry to hear about your wife's death last year."

"Thank you. It was a hard blow for all of us."

"I guess that's why we haven't heard much from you lately. I do tell people about your ranch from time to time. It's a shame it isn't better known."

Kelly verbally bounded into this gap. "I've been encouraging Diego to hold an open house with tours of the ranch and riding demonstrations. If you thought his horses looked impressive on parade, you should see them actually perform!"

To Diego's chagrin, Weimer lit up at this prospect. "Sounds like a wonderful idea! Let me know when you're holding it, and I'll run an announcement in the Historical Society bulletin."

"We haven't really decided yet," Diego told him, "but thank you." Trying to be subtle, he steered Kelly away. Then he asked her in a whisper, "Why did you have to mention the open house? I haven't made up my mind about that yet."

She threw him the impish smile. "I just wanted you to see how much he would like the idea. This is a political event, so I figured I'd do some campaigning of my own."

He was about to argue further when he glimpsed someone looking pointedly in their direction—a tall man, gray at the temples, with tanned, sharp, patrician features, and wearing a subdued madras blazer.

Kelly recognized him at the same time. "Isn't that Gavin Thorne?"

This took Diego by surprise. "How do you know him?"

She hesitated. "I told you, Fisher & Lyons promotes his resort. I've seen his picture."

While Diego was still deciding whether or not to speak to his renowned neighbor, Thorne approached him. "Villaneuva, this is a surprise! I don't often see you out at events like this."

"I'm turning over a new leaf." Responding to Thorne's handshake, Diego added, "I'm surprised to see you here, too. I would think some of Brooks' proposals might run contrary to your interests."

"Hey, I'm just another farmer like the rest of you—got my agri-school diploma to prove it!" he joked. "Truth is, I have a stretch of undeveloped property back behind the golf courses that qualifies as a mini nature preserve. It's the most godawful rocky slope, but it's got some rare species of lizard—got some long, Latin name. Anyway, it would entitle me to a tax break under this new open spaces bill Brooks is proposing."

"Amazing." Diego told himself it was true what they said—the rich got richer. They knew how to work all the angles

"It's obvious why you're here, of course," Thorne went on. "I know he's also promoting tax credits for farmers and ranchers. I'm sure you can use any help you can get, eh?"

Because Thorne sounded sympathetic, Diego didn't take offense. "We're doing all right these days. A lot of the credit goes to Kelly here." Diego introduced her, explained her business background and told Thorne how she'd improved the web site.

Thorne studied Kelly, who appeared unruffled by his scrutiny. "Where did you work in public relations?"

When she told him, he seemed impressed. "Good firm. Wally Lyons has done some fine work for me over the years."

He addressed Diego again, with a smile. "I admire your determination. I'm sure it's a hard way to make a living, raising horses. Even a Kentucky thoroughbred farm is always a crapshoot. And you're dealing with a breed hardly anyone here has heard of, with very specialized talents—"

Kelly piped up brightly. "That's exactly what we intend to promote, of course. The rarity of the breed and its amazing, inborn gifts for dressage."

Thorne gave a sharp laugh, and told Diego, "She sounds like your secret weapon, all right. Well, best of luck to you!"

That ended their conversation, and Diego breathed easier. At least this time around Thorne hadn't made a pitch to buy him out.

The extra weight in his blazer pocket reminded him of the new cell phone stashed there. It had remained mute so far, so he trusted everything was still quiet back at the ranch.

A robust man with a bad comb-over, in a blue seersucker suit, took to the dais and tapped the microphone. He introduced himself as Colin McPherson, editor of the *Sun*. After a few glowing words about the candidate, he turned the podium over to Brooks.

*   *   *

As she listened to Brooks speak, Kelly paid almost as much attention to McPherson. Now, there was someone she needed to collar! Diego might not approve, but when would they get an opportunity like this again?

Brooks eventually finished and they all applauded. Then Diego played right into Kelly's hands by offering to get her another white wine. She watched him fight his way to the bar at the rear of the room, then intercepted McPherson on his way down from the dais.

She talked up the ranch. McPherson knew little about Rancho Villaneuva and sounded intrigued. Once again, Kelly floated the idea of the open house, and suggested a preview story might drum up interest.

"Send me some background on the place," McPherson said. "I'll think it over."

"Great!" Kelly thought of the old but still relevant brochures lying around the barn office. She could write a letter to update them, and refer McPherson to the newer information on the web site. She wondered if Diego would go along with a newspaper interview.

She scanned the room until she spotted his head full of black waves. He hadn't made much progress in returning from the bar. Kelly saw him talking with someone...

Someone wearing a spanking-white Western hat. Not unlike the one she'd found in the *arroyo*.

Cautiously, Kelly made her way in Diego's direction. She stayed in his blind spot until she'd a chance to check out his conversational partner. The curvy blonde overdid her appeal with beauty queen hair and makeup, and a white Western-style dress that dripped fringe at the sleeves and hem. Even her high-heeled, lace-up boots were white.

Kelly remained fixated, though, on the hat. She remembered Helga saying the one from the *arroyo* could belong to a woman with a large head.

Or one with a big hairdo.

Kelly hardly needed to ask the identity of this Annie Oakley character. She figured it had to be Sandy Garrett. The blond woman lived up to everything Helga and the Martinezes had said about her, in both looks and behavior. Patting Diego's injured side with one of her brightly manicured hands, and clucking over him like a mother hen, Sandy threw signals only a blind and deaf man could've missed. In her other hand, she held a nearly full glass of white wine. *The one Diego got for me,* suspected Kelly.

She told herself wryly that was the last straw. She had to interrupt this mating game, even if it were totally one-sided.

Sandy shot her a disdainful look before even finding out who she was. She would've done the same, Kelly figured, to any interloping female. When Diego greeted Kelly with enthusiasm, and maybe even a note of relief, that seemed to irritate Sandy even further. But to her credit, she struggled to hide it.

"Diego was just telling me about the awful fire you had last weekend," she said. "Lucky he didn't lose any of the horses."

Diego laughed. "After Hidalgo knocked me down, Kelly threw herself in front of him to keep him from running away."

Kelly noticed that, this time around, he sounded more bragging than angry about her behavior. She told Sandy, "Diego risked his life to save both horses. It was like something out of a movie."

"I wish I'd been there to see it." Sandy turned her admiring gaze on Diego again. "But it's a shame you got hurt in the process."

"Aah, a couple more weeks and I'll be good as new." He seemed half-flattered and half-embarrassed by all the female attention. This surprised Kelly. Most handsome men would be used to women fawning over them. Maybe it was a good thing, in some ways, that he kept himself sequestered on his ranch most of the time!

"Still," continued Sandy, "you're going to be short-handed now. Helga and Kelly can only do so much. Listen, do you want me to keep the stallions over at the Lucky Shot until the repairs are done? My stud barn has a couple of empty stalls."

Diego shook his head. "Thanks, but I don't think that'll be necessary. So far, the electric fencing has kept them in their paddocks. Repairs on the barn start next week, so that shouldn't take long."

Sandy nodded gravely. "I hope you're taking some precautions against this happening again."

Before Kelly could head him off, Diego explained all about the new security system. Sandy tried to sell him on a few additional options she had at her ranch, but Diego felt they were too expensive for him to consider at the moment.

Sandy smiled. "Well, if you ever want somebody to keep an eye on the place while you're out, I'll be glad to come over and bring my rifle. I'd love to get a bead on the varmint who's been sabotaging you. And I'd nail him, too! Last exhibition I gave upstate, I hit a golf ball in mid-air at twenty-five yards."

Kelly could only hope the woman was kidding, and wouldn't actually shoot an interloper on sight. "Maybe you should work out a deal with Gavin Thorne. He could use some livelier entertainment over at Rio Dorado—and he's got a lot of golf balls. He could hit 'em and you could shoot 'em!"

At first, Sandy didn't seem to appreciate Kelly chiming in with a joke and momentarily stealing the attention. When Diego laughed, though, Sandy did, too. "Thorne's got a lot of balls, period!" Turning back to Diego, she squeezed his arm protectively again. "Really, I'm worried about you. First, the poisoning, and now this...I mean, someone who'll burn down a building doesn't care who gets hurt, animals or people. Next time, they might go after you directly." As an afterthought, she glanced at Kelly. "Or one of your staff."

"We're all on the alert," Diego assured her. "One of these days, we may even nail the 'varmint.' But thanks for your concern."

"If I can help in any way, just let me know."

Diego noted then that, speaking of such things, he and Kelly should probably get back to the ranch. Even then, he nearly had to pry Sandy's long, rosy nails from his navy-blue gabardine sleeve to make an escape.

As they headed for the door, he told Kelly, "I still owe you a wine. I'll pour you one when we get back to the house."

"I can do without it. I still have some horses to exercise this afternoon." Kelly tried to be tactful with her next comment. "Maybe you shouldn't spread it around too much, Diego, about the new security system. For those electric-eye things to work, the intruder shouldn't know they're there."

He looked astonished. "I didn't spread it around. I only told Sandy."

"Mmm. But she might just tell somebody who might tell somebody...and eventually, it could get back to the person who's been playing these dirty tricks. After all, we have no idea who that is, but it's somebody close enough to know a lot about you and the operations of your ranch."

Diego seemed to appreciate the sense of this, but still countered, "Sandy won't say anything to anyone. She may act a little—how d'you say?—head-in-the-air—"

"Air-headed."

Diego acknowledged the correction with a sharp nod. "But she's really very shrewd. I don't mind her knowing what's been going on. She might even help us catch the guy!"

Silently, Kelly added, *Unless the "guy" is Sandy herself!*

Maybe that was unfair. Maybe she was just feeling jealous over Diego. But Sandy could have lost that hat at the bottom of the *arroyo*. If she did, Kelly had to wonder what the blond sharpshooter had been doing down there.

Helga said Sandy had her eye on Diego, even while he was still married. How badly, Kelly wondered, had she wanted him?

Badly enough to dispose of Isabella?

CHAPTER 13

To Kelly's relief, Diego didn't object to the idea of the *Sun* doing a story on Rancho Villaneuva. He even seemed to soften towards the open house idea, as if getting so much positive feedback at the fundraiser had given him more confidence in the future.

Helga also warmed to the prospect of a newspaper article. She told Kelly, "The *Sun* did one on us five or six years ago, while Diego's father was alive. I've got it in our files." She retrieved it from the barn office.

It was a fairly short piece, and the male reporter had gotten a couple of things wrong, obviously misunderstanding some of the statements by Bernardo and Diego. Still, it had a striking photo of Basilio in a *levade* with Diego's father aboard, and another of Hidalgo as a two-year-old. The wiry, clean-shaven man who held the lead line was identified in the caption as "Head groom Rico Farley."

Kelly peered more closely. So this was the guy who had caused so much heartache! He looked pretty nondescript, although something about his bearing struck her as vaguely familiar. The newspaper photo was grainy, though, and he wore a baseball-type cap that half-shadowed his face, so she couldn't fix her impression on anything in particular.

*   *   *

Work on the stallion barn began the following Monday. Diego supervised, meanwhile grumbling that if it weren't for his rib, he,

93

Alonzo and Felipe probably could have done the whole job for a lot less.

Helga gently reminded him that everyone had a specialty. "You need Alonzo and Felipe to take care of the horses. Might as well let the construction guys do what they do best."

The barn and Diego's rib healed at about the same rate. Both were nearly mended when a reporter from the *Sun,* Chloe Fleming, called to make an appointment.

Kelly heard Diego on the office phone inviting Chloe out the following Tuesday. Once he hung up, she asked him, "Do you think that's too soon? I know the doctor told you not to ride for another week. I was hoping they could get some pictures of you and Hidalgo in action."

"Don't worry," he told her, mysteriously. "I'll see that they get all the action pictures they could possibly want!"

*   *   *

Chloe looked nothing like her glamorous name. A stocky, fortyish woman with bushy brown hair, she wore round, wire glasses that unfortunately echoed the shape of her face, a long purple sundress and flat sandals. After welcoming her, Kelly warned of the potential hazards she faced in open-toed shoes, such as manure or an ill-placed hoof. Chloe just shrugged and said she had grown up on a farm with horses. Kelly liked her instantly for her lack of prissiness.

Tagging after her came an acned photographer named Steve, who looked half Chloe's age. He wore jeans and a Rams T-shirt, and chewed gum as if it had become one of his natural, physical functions. Kelly got the impression he normally covered sports. She doubted his experience included anything as rarified as horse shows.

At the main barn, Diego took over the tour with aplomb, even seeming to enjoy himself. He explained to his visitors that the Andalusian dated back to about 700 A.D.; that for centuries it was the favored horse in all the royal courts of Europe; that it was the chief progenitor of the famous Lipizzaner breed, and a strong influence upon many others, including the American Quarter Horse.

He pointed out the various mares—Chloe oohed and aahed, especially over Belleza—and let Steve photograph Helga with little Paco, always a charmer. Kelly led Gitano from his stall so Diego could use him to point out the breed's typical characteristics. Meanwhile, Gitano played goodwill ambassador, cheerfully allowing Chloe to stroke his nose and run her fingers through his luxuriant, wavy mane.

Helga slipped up behind Kelly and handed her a long dressage whip. "If you really want to impress them," she said, "touch him on the shoulder with this."

Kelly, not sure what to expect, followed orders. Right in the barn aisle, Gitano sank into a deep, gentlemanly bow, bending one knee and sliding the other front leg forward. When Kelly removed the whip, he sprang upright again, his nearest eye gleaming from under his heavy forelock with a sense of fun.

Chloe clapped in delight, and Diego laughed aloud. "I'd almost forgotten he could do that!"

"Gitano the Wonder Horse!" announced Kelly. At Steve's request, they repeated the move outside in the sunshine, so he could get a good shot.

They moved on, then, to the stallion barn. Diego explained briefly about the recent fire, which he made sound purely accidental. While he apologized for not being able to ride, Felipe brought Hidalgo out on long reins.

Hmmm, thought Kelly, intrigued. *Wonder what Diego's got up his sleeve?*

Steve shrank back a little. "Is that the same one that busted your rib?"

"That wasn't his fault. You'd get upset, too, if your hair caught on fire." Taking the reins, Diego asked, "How fast is your film?"

When Steve told him it was the same speed he used to shoot a basketball game, Diego invited him along into the outdoor ring. "Just stay back near the fence."

Steve, an obvious city boy, needed no further warning. Kelly figured, though, that Diego wasn't concerned about the stallion misbehaving. He just didn't want Steve in the way once the horse started doing his thing properly.

Diego walked behind Hidalgo with the long reins, sometimes also signaling him with a lunge whip. First he put the horse into a Spanish Walk, in which Hidalgo kicked forward dramatically with each foreleg before setting it down. Then the stallion went through the same movements he had performed with Diego on his back, the day Kelly had first seen them—the slow, rhythmic trot or *passage*; the high-stepping trot in place, or *piaffe*; and the statuesque rear, balancing on the haunches, or *levade*. Hidalgo performed flawlessly, snorting now and then as if he enjoyed showing off.

"That's great!" said Chloe. Next to Kelly, on the rail, she scribbled in her spiral notepad. "What do you call that last move?"

A glance at the notepad told Kelly the reporter had gotten the first two terms right—she knew something about basic dressage. Kelly spelled *levade* for Chloe.

Then both of them realized they should've kept their eyes on the ring. Hidalgo reared again, but this time he hopped forward on his hind legs. Once—twice—three times, before his front legs touched down again.

"Wow!" Chloe said. "What was that?"

Kelly had to search her memory for the term. "*Courbette,* I think. I didn't even know he could do that!"

That display almost prepared Kelly for what was to follow. Hidalgo danced a little on the long lines, excited, until Diego calmed him with a few words in Spanish. At another "*Arriba!*" from his master, he squatted as before—then leaped high into the air, and kicked straight backward with his hind legs. He landed nimbly and shook his full mane in macho pride.

"*Capriole,*" Kelly told Chloe, a bit awestruck herself.

"Unbelievable! I thought they only did that stuff at the Spanish Riding School."

Kelly laughed. "Before there were Lipizzaners, they did it with Andalusians. Why do you think it's called the Spanish Riding School?"

"I never thought of that." Visibly impressed, Chloe made a few more notes.

Diego asked Felipe to walk the stallion for a few minutes before putting him away. As Steve left the ring, Chloe told him, "I hope you got those shots!"

The photographer nodded. "I'm glad he told me to use the fast film—and to stand by the fence. That horse has one hell of a karate kick!"

Kelly grinned. "Originally, cavalry horses were taught to do that to clobber the foot soldiers. Nasty trick, eh?"

When Diego joined them, Chloe congratulated him on his nerve.

He played down any danger. "Hidalgo's my buddy, and he'd never hurt me—not on purpose. I just have to know where to stand!"

They wound up in the barn office, where he gave the visitors some more written background on the ranch, his father, and the Royal Andalusian School in Spain. Asked when he planned his open house, Diego hesitated. "Probably some time in July. As soon as we firm up the date, we'll let you know."

Kelly listened in wonder. He was actually committing himself—sort of. This thing might happen after all! For the moment, she didn't even worry about pulling it off. She felt as if the hardest part was over—convincing Diego.

By the time Chloe and Steve finally left, it was late afternoon. Some minor chores had gone undone, but no one fussed about them. Kelly, Diego and Helga were all too up.

"I liked the fact that Chloe already knew a little about horses," said Kelly.

"Yeah," said Helga. "With luck, she won't make the same kind of mistakes as the reporter who wrote the first story."

That reminded Kelly of something that had been nagging at her and she turned to Diego. "You mentioned you have some old videos of you and your father working with the horses. Could I see them sometime?"

"Sure...I guess so. I can pull them out tonight after dinner, if you want."

"That would be great."

She let him think she was merely curious. No point in upsetting him unnecessarily.

Time enough for that if the tapes bore out her worst suspicions.

*   *   *

The only t.v. in Diego's part of the house was in the rear sunroom which doubled as a kind of family room. Felipe had just settled in to watch one of the *Halloween* sequels on cable when Diego and Kelly moved him out. He was a good sport about it, but expressed some doubts about his parents letting him watch a horror movie in their wing of the house.

"If they don't, check back with us in about an hour, " said Diego. "We might be done with the videos by then."

He stooped by an old, leather-bound trunk to search through the tapes stored there. Meanwhile, Kelly nestled against the flowered cushions of the dark wicker sofa. She liked the solarium for its tropical atmosphere. Big plants clustered beneath the deep, filigreed windows on three sides, and a ceiling fan made the most of the evening's faint breeze. After a day of wearing long pants and boots to work around the horses, both she and Diego had changed into comfortable shorts and T-shirts.

Straightening up near the trunk, Diego held out three videotapes.

"What do you want to see? We have an early one we made of Basilio when we first put him up for stud, one from about five years back of his first crop of foals, and one from the year before my father died. I think the last one has some show and parade footage, too."

Kelly wondered which was most likely to tell her what she needed to know. "I guess the most recent one."

Until the tape began, she hadn't considered the down side of her request.

The professional-looking video opened with footage of Basilio galloping free in the field, his hawk-like profile cleaving the wind, his white mane and tail blowing out behind him. The voice that narrated sounded like Diego's, but with a heavier accent and a rougher timbre that might come with age. *Bernardo,* Kelly thought. She wondered if Diego had watched this tape at all since his father's death. If not, it might be rough on him emotionally. She hadn't intended that.

The elder *Señor* Villanueva recited Basilio's regal Spanish bloodlines and the various honors he had earned at shows in both his homeland and in the U.S. Cut to Hidalgo, then a frisky three-year-old, while Bernardo extolled the physical and temperamental virtues the sire had passed on to his colt.

Next, Bernardo appeared in full Spanish costume riding Basilio in front of an audience, probably at some breed show. Then came a brief segment with all three riders in a local parade—Bernardo, Diego and Isabella.

The brunette beauty wore the same white dress with the red-trimmed ruffles as in the picture Kelly had seen in the barn office. Riding sidesaddle with ease, she held her reins in one hand and used the other to wave to parade watchers gathered on the curb. In action, she exuded even more warmth and charm than in her still photos.

Kelly swallowed hard. She wondered if that gray mare, red ribbons braided through her mane, was the same one that had tossed Isabella to her death in the *arroyo.* From the look of the video, the horse had tolerated the noise and activity of the parade with no problems. What, out in the middle of the desert, could have made her spook so violently?

Diego finally spoke up, his voice thick with emotion. "We can fast forward through some of this."

Kelly glanced over and saw a sheen in his dark eyes. "I'm sorry. I didn't realize there would be so much of your father and Isabella. I didn't mean to make you sad all over again."

He sighed. "You know, I deliberately haven't watched any of these tapes because I didn't think I could stand to. But now I'm glad I have them. I must be making progress. I can appreciate them now as good memories."

Kelly reached over to squeeze his free hand. "I'm glad. That does sound like progress."

The video had moved on to show horses for sale at the time. "I don't know if you care about this part," said Diego. "We sold a lot of these guys. And the mares...well, you know what happened to most of them."

Each animal was brought out and led around for the video, usually by Diego or Helga. When a wiry man in a baseball cap brought out one colt and halted it in front of the camera, Kelly suddenly focused more sharply. "There he is! Can you wind that back again?"

Diego looked confused. "Why? We sold that colt two years ago."

"Not the colt, the guy leading him."

To oblige her, Diego rewound two or three minutes of tape and replayed them. For a few seconds, the camera panned over the man's narrow, clean-shaven, tanned face and captured his grin, with a flash of gold halfway back on the right side.

In a disgusted tone, Diego told her, "That's just Rico Farley."

"It's also Eddie Hernandez!"

Diego froze the onscreen image with the pause button and gaped at Kelly. "The guy you found prowling around here the day you started work?"

She nodded. "I thought I recognized him in the old newspaper photo, but I needed to see him closer up and moving around to be sure. Hernandez had a moustache and fancier clothes, but the same hair, build and walk—even the same gold tooth!"

Diego slumped back against the sofa cushions, his gaze still fixed on the fuzzy electronic likeness of his former groom. "He just gave you a phony name. And made up a story to explain what he was doing here."

"He didn't leave a number 'cause he had no real interest in buying a horse. I probably surprised him right after he stuck the oleander into the hay bales." Kelly remembered something else. "And he didn't drive into the barnyard because he didn't want anyone to see him coming or going."

Diego frowned. "We would've recognized his truck, if he's still driving the same one. He had an old red Ford pickup with one gray door on the cab. Y'know, primed—he never got around to repainting it."

Just then, Felipe put his head back in the solarium door. Shyly, as if he thought he might be interrupting something private between Kelly and Diego. When he saw that he wasn't, he asked, "Are you done watching videos? I might still have time to see if Jamie Lee Curtis gets away from Jason."

With a tight smile, Diego gestured towards the tv screen. "I've got a better one for you—Kelly just figured out who's been trying to drive us out of business."

Felipe gawked at the still-paused image of Rico Farley.

Kelly couldn't resist adding a touch of *Halloween*-style melodrama. "He's ba-a-ack!"

CHAPTER 14

The next morning, after breakfast, Diego brainstormed with his staff about this new information. Alonzo thought they should go to the police, but Diego pointed out they still had no real evidence to link Farley to either the poisoned hay or the barn fire.

"We've already increased our security measures," he said. "I think all we can do from here on is keep our eyes open. At least now we know who we're looking for—Rico Farley with a new moustache."

Helga looked grave. "With any luck, he won't try anything more. Or if he does, we'll catch him red-handed."

In some ways, it seemed logical to Kelly that Rico was behind the sabotage. He had an intimate knowledge of the farm and a grudge against Diego. Still, she felt some element was missing. After all, Rico had killed Diego's wife—if only indirectly—and not the other way around. Why such a bloody vendetta?

"I guess he found out you blackballed him with all the other farms around here," she suggested to Diego. "When he couldn't find work, he held it against you. But why didn't he just go somewhere else, out of state or even across the border? Wouldn't that have been easier than hanging around just to make your life miserable?"

Helga answered for her boss. "Rico never was the brightest bulb in the pack. And he's lazy. Maybe looking for other honest work was too much trouble for him."

Kelly considered this. "He must've found something, though. When I met him, he was wearing fancy Western clothes. Embroidered shirt, tooled belt with a big silver buckle, snakeskin boots. Even his sunglasses looked like the designer kind."

"Maybe he's selling drugs," piped up Felipe. When his mother shot him a startled look, the boy added, "He offered me weed a couple of times. If he'd do that, he could be dealing the stuff. Or even something harder."

Kelly thought of the joint she'd found under her mattress. Yes, something like that could explain Rico's apparently healthy income, maybe even his new criminal inclinations.

Diego slapped both hands flat on the trestle table in front of him. "If we can forget about Farley for the moment, we have another matter to discuss. Kelly has told the newspaper we're going to have an open house, so I guess we'd better start making plans."

After their initial surprise, everyone dove in to contribute ideas. It was decided Diego would perform on Hidalgo and Kelly on Gitano. Diego also would show off Belleza, Helga would bring out Turi, and Felipe would jump—"Low jumps!" his mother insisted—on Basilio. Alonzo would help groom and tack up the horses, and Nora would organize refreshments.

During the general chatter, Kelly told Diego quietly, "I'm so glad you're going ahead with it. I thought finding out about Rico might discourage you."

"It almost did," he admitted. "But after I thought about it, I decided we can't operate in fear. Now that I know Rico is behind this, I want to catch him! In fact, I want you to publicize the open house as much as possible."

"Oh?"

"If Farley wants to ruin my business, and he sees we're planning a big event, that could flush him out and make him reckless. Then all he has to do is make one slip—" Diego smiled darkly "—and we'll grab him!"

* * *

Although he still couldn't ride Hidalgo for a few more days, Diego began seriously coaching Kelly. He'd helped her in the past when she worked with the younger or more difficult horses, but normally left her on her own to ride Gitano, confident neither would do the other any harm. Now, however, she needed to put on a show for an audience and had to sharpen her moves accordingly.

It impressed Diego how far she'd already come with her favorite horse. They obviously had developed a real partnership, so that the freckled gelding responded quickly to her slightest cues. Kelly already knew how to do a flying lead change—a shift in the horse's balance at the canter that looked like a skipping step. Diego taught her to signal with her legs more crisply so Gitano would change every fourth stride, then every third stride, until he really appeared to be dancing. He also showed her how to execute the move he'd done on Hidalgo the first morning they met—the *passage* into *piaffe*.

Kelly showed obvious delight in learning how to do these higher-level movements on a horse already well-trained for them. Of course, Gitano was middle-aged and hadn't done anything quite so strenuous in a few years, but he obviously tried his heart out for Kelly. Diego realized more than ever that she had real talent and the potential to become a top horsewoman.

Hard to say whether she's wasting her head for business by working here, he thought, *or whether she was wasting her riding skills all those years by working in an office!*

*   *   *

The article in the *Sun* came out that Thursday, and was everything they could have hoped for. Chloe got all her information straight, and showed a flair in her writing unusual for a reporter at a small, weekly paper. The story ran with two good photos—Gitano bowing for Kelly, and Hidalgo kicking out as he hovered high above the ground in his *capriole*. The article mentioned, towards the end, that Rancho Villaneuva planned an open house some time that summer, with the date to be announced.

Once the item appeared, Diego got phone calls from people he hadn't heard from in years, as well as from fellow members of the ranchers' association. Most congratulated him on the great publicity and said they would try to get to the open house. The only caller who sounded a note of caution was Sandy Garrett.

"Do you really think it's a good idea to plan such a public event when you may have somebody...stalking you? Or at least your horses?"

"I'm not so worried about that anymore." Diego told her whom he suspected of doing all the damage so far.

He heard a beat of surprised silence on the line. "Rico Farley? I thought he'd left the area!"

"We all just assumed that, but apparently he's still hanging around.

Actually, Kelly was the one who figured it out." After Diego explained how, that chill crept into Sandy's voice again. It always seemed to, Diego noticed, whenever he praised Kelly.

"Well, that was clever of her! Still, just because you know it's Farley doesn't mean he can't strike again."

Why did she always have to be so negative? Diego thought he knew the answer. Sandy wanted him to need her, and it annoyed her to think he didn't. "Let me worry about that, Sandy. But there is one thing you can do to help."

"Anything!"

"You know what Farley looks like—you saw him helping us at the horse shows. Just add a moustache and you've got the new picture. Anyway, he's got to be living, and maybe even working, somewhere around here. So in your travels, keep an eye out, okay?"

"I surely will. And when I spot the toad and he tries to run, I promise I'll put a bullet in his leg to slow him down!"

Though he did try to discourage her itchy trigger finger, Diego hung up thinking it was nice to have two feisty women on his side.

*   *   *

Late the next morning, while Kelly was lunging Turi, Diego returned from the doctor's minus the bulging bandage under his shirt. Smiling, he patted his rib cage to emphasize his liberation.

"Congratulations!" Kelly let the colt slow to a walk. "How do you plan to celebrate?"

"How else? After three weeks, I'm going for a ride! Want to join me?"

She glanced towards the horse she'd been exercising. "I thought I had a lot of work to do today."

"It can wait a few hours. Saddle up your pal Gitano, and we'll go kick up some dust."

"You're the boss!"

Kelly felt flattered. She hadn't seen Diego go for many rides in the open country—probably, he'd been too busy for such recreation—and when he did, he always went alone. Obviously, he was feeling buzzed over finally having gotten rid of his bandage.

*   *   *

As they set out together, another thought occurred to Kelly. She wondered if Diego had ever gone riding this way, for fun, with anyone except his late wife.

Forget it, she told herself. *Don't spoil things by obsessing over Isabella. If he's starting to get over her death, so can you!*

Kelly felt more relaxed riding side-by-side with Diego than she did in the ring with him giving the orders and her struggling to carry them out. She wondered if this meant he was starting to think of her as more of an equal. Diego also had a different, more carefree air about him today. In his chambray shirt, and riding one-handed, he looked less like a spit-and-polish dressage trainer and more like a dashing Latino cowboy.

They reached a flat, open stretch and he threw out a sudden challenge. "Race you to that big boulder!"

"They're not racehorses, Diego."

"They don't know that. *Uno...dos...tres!*"

Hidalgo leaped forward in a dusty explosion. With little urging from Kelly, Gitano took off after him.

In fact, it startled Kelly how much speed her mid-mannered mount held in reserve. Carried along by the surge of raw, animal power, she yelled into Gitano's ear, "Hee-ya, let's catch those guys!"

She could feel the horse's big muscles churning and hear his snorts of excitement, as he tried his best. Hidalgo, though, had the edge in terms of youth and testosterone; they chased his flying gray tail and star-spangled rump in vain. He and Diego skidded to a stop at the boulder several lengths ahead of Gitano and Kelly.

"Like that was a fair contest!" she grumbled. "Your horse still has *cojones.*"

Diego laughed out loud. "How did a nice Irish-American girl learn a word like that?"

"Ha! From two years living in a marginal neighborhood in L.A."

They rode on almost shoulder-to-shoulder, and he nudged her with his elbow. "I thought you had enough *cojones* for the both of you!"

Kelly blushed, not sure if that was a compliment or not. "Well, we Irish-American girls do have that reputation. But at least I never got into sharpshooting."

"Good thing. You might be even more dangerous than Sandy Garrett."

Kelly almost tossed a remark back, but held her tongue. She considered telling him about the crushed hat she'd found in the arroyo. There was a time when she'd strongly suspected the hat belonged to Sandy. In her mind, Kelly had sketched out a dark scenario in which

Sandy had secretly ambushed Isabella, maybe even fired off a shot close enough to spook Isabella's horse and cause her fatal fall.

By now, though, Kelly had decided the pearl-gray hat belonged to Rico Farley. Maybe he'd lost it on one of his clandestine visits to Rancho Villaneuva. Perhaps he drove in a back way and concealed his too-recognizable truck in the *arroyo* while he did his dirty work. Kelly reminded herself she really had no idea how long the hat had laid buried there—it might've been only a couple of months.

Anyway, now that they knew Rico was the bad guy, there was no reason to suspect anyone else. Much as she might dislike Sandy, Kelly couldn't accuse her of anything more than being a tough cookie a little too accustomed to getting her own way.

At that point, Kelly and Diego found their peaceful ramble interrupted by a drone from above. Kelly shielded her eyes to look up and saw a golden helicopter glinting in the midday sun. "Don't tell me—Gavin Thorne!"

Diego laughed again. "Good guess. What gave it away, the gold color? For Rio Dorado?"

"That, and the fact I know he has a helicopter pad at the resort. In fact, I understand his pilot is something of a lush, so we'd better hope the bird stays up there."

Diego stared at her. "You know more than I do! Where did you hear that about the pilot?"

"I saw him half in the bag at lunchtime a couple of weeks ago, over in the Twilight Lounge."

The black eyes narrowed at her. "And what were you doing there at lunchtime?"

"Tracking down the source of that matchbook. And trying to find out if Neal had been in there the day before. The bartender hadn't seen him. Too bad I didn't know enough back then to ask about Rico Farley!"

The low-hovering copter started to wear on Hidalgo's nerves. He sidestepped, bumping into Gitano, who took the insult in stride. Diego calmed the stallion, but told Kelly, "Let's dismount until that thing goes away. After what you said about the pilot, I don't trust him either."

They hand-walked the horses to a rise that overlooked the grounds of Rio Dorado, and watched the chopper gradually circle back in that direction.

Diego asked Kelly, "You actually went over to that lounge to try to prove your friend's innocence? You must still care for him."

This interpretation took her by surprise. "Not…in that way. I mean, it's true I didn't believe he was capable of starting the fire on purpose. But also, I didn't want you to think he and I were involved in some kind of conspiracy against you."

Diego shook his head. It took Kelly a minute to realize the person he was rebuking was himself. "I know I gave you a pretty hard time, Kelly, over the past couple of months. I have no excuse, except…I guess the sabotage, coming just a year after Isabella's death, made me feel like the whole world was against me."

She nodded. "I can certainly understand that."

"I had almost decided to give up and sell the ranch. When you came here with so much enthusiasm, you made me hope again."

"I guess the fire made you feel as if you'd been stupid to get your hopes up. Maybe even stupid to trust me."

He faced Kelly with more urgent emotion in his eyes than he ever had dared to show her before. "I was wrong. I should never have suspected you. You've done so much for this ranch in just the short time you've been here…and for me."

Kelly felt her cheeks warm again, and tried to make light of her contributions. "Shucks, no, I haven't. A little tinkering with the web site, a little schmoozing with the newspaper editor—"

"I don't mean just those things. You've made this place feel alive again. I was dragging everybody down with my brooding. The others were too polite, I guess, to tell me to stop feeling sorry for myself. You made me remember I have something here worth fighting for."

Kelly's throat tightened with conflicted feelings. He was giving her too much credit, she believed, and selling himself short. "You don't need me to give you courage. You've obviously had that all along. You came to a strange country as a very young man, survived your father's death and Isabella's, and built up this business without any help from me. If you got discouraged by the idea that some unknown person was trying to destroy everything you'd worked for…Well, who wouldn't? Maybe you just needed some help to get over that rough spot."

"You did help me, and I'm grateful…"

The hand he rested on Kelly's shoulder gradually slipped around her waist. Kelly had no thought of resisting as she melted into his arms. For a moment, she gazed mesmerized into those deep, dark eyes before she felt his strong, warm mouth close upon hers.

She'd spent so much effort talking herself out of her desire that it came as a shock now to realize this was what she wanted, more than anything. She glided her arms around him in return, and relished the feel of the iron muscles in his back, the sweet scent of his perspiration mingling with her own.

By the time they parted, Diego's color had deepened a shade, and it wasn't from sunburn. "I probably shouldn't have done that."

Kelly smiled. "If anyone complains, I'll take at least half the blame."

"Oh, really?" He relaxed, finally understanding that she returned his feelings. "I'm glad you aren't still carrying the torch for Neal. Isn't that the expression?"

She nodded. "No torch. Not even a matchbook."

Diego winced at her bad joke, but it didn't stop him from kissing her again. Kelly began to respond a bit more passionately this time...when suddenly she felt him lose his balance and half-stumble out of her embrace.

He glared at his horse. Hidalgo, growing bored and sighting a patch of grass not far away, had yanked the reins and attempted to drag his master in that direction. Diego snapped back on the reins, but the punishment was mild and his frown twisted with humor. "Maybe we should resume this some other time, when Junior isn't around to interrupt."

"He's just jealous. He's used to having your full attention."

"He's going to have to adjust his thinking."

They mounted again and rode back along the rise, with the grounds of Rio Dorado still sprawled below them. Diego pointed to an arid stretch on the far side. "I wonder why Thorne wants my property at all? If he needs to expand, he has plenty of land over there."

"Remember what he said at the fundraiser, about having his own little nature preserve? The rare type of lizard that turned up on his property? Maybe that's the area. If he wants his open spaces tax credit, he can't build there."

"I forgot about that. You're probably right." All at once, Diego halted his horse and peered more intently down the slope. "Hold on a minute. I want to see something."

He steered Hidalgo down the rocky incline. Just below stretched a cluster of Spanish-style bungalows, rental units for those who wanted, and could afford, more luxury and privacy than just a hotel room. Following him, Kelly could see the buildings were beautifully landscaped with white, flowering bushes flanking the all doorways.

They rode on until a hurricane fence, half-concealed by shrubbery, kept them from going any further.

"Hard to tell from here," said Kelly, "but don't those bushes look like—"

"Oleander," Diego finished, in a taut voice. "I never even noticed before. Rio Dorado is crawling with it."

CHAPTER 15

Back in the stable yard, Diego and Kelly told Helga about their latest discovery.

She asked them, "But how would Farley have gotten the oleander from Rio Dorado? I can't see him just tearing handfuls off the bushes without somebody stopping him."

Diego shrugged. "They have so many gardeners over there, they probably prune those bushes once a week. He could have offered to cart the leaves away, maybe even slipped somebody a few dollars for the privilege. Who would say no?"

"And," Kelly pointed out, "they'd be clippings—bits and pieces—just right for mixing in with the hay."

"That's probably just how it happened." Helga's mouth twisted bitterly. "For a small-time horse groom with no money, Farley seems to spend a lot of time at Rio Dorado!"

Diego's expression turned keen again. "He does, doesn't he? In fact, I'm going to call Mr. Gavin Thorne right now, explain our problem, and ask him to keep a lookout for Farley. Maybe he can tell his employees to do the same."

"Not a bad idea," said Kelly. "If he needs to know what Farley looks like, I'll fax him the old newspaper photo. I can even draw a moustache on it first!"

*   *   *

Although Thorne did maintain an office at Rio Dorado, Diego's call got him only as far as the man's assistant. She said Mr. Thorne would be away for a few days, scouting out new ventures.

Diego knew better than to leave a complicated message with the assistant. "Please ask him to call me as soon as he gets back."

Standing next to him in the barn office, Kelly told Diego, "When he hears that, he'll think you've finally decided to sell."

"Good. That might make him call me back faster." He turned to her with a smile and rested both hands on her shoulders. "Now, don't you and I have some unfinished business to get back to?"

"I can't imagine what!" she purred, nestling into his arms. "Oh, that's right—I still have to work out my routine for the open house."

He laughed out loud. "And they call me a workaholic! That wasn't the unfinished business I had in mind." He glanced around broadly. "I don't see Hidalgo anywhere, do you?"

"I think he's safely locked up."

Diego seized the opportunity to kiss her again. This time he showed far more determination, taking her firmly by the shoulders and massaging them in a way that sent the mercury in her personal thermometer shooting skyward. His tongue teased her lips apart, then gently tickled and stroked her own, setting all those banked embers in her heart suddenly ablaze.

Kelly pressed tightly against him in surrender, until alarm bells started to clang in her head. As she breathlessly pushed herself back from his hard chest, she reflected that Diego finally seemed to be recovering from his long depression over Isabella!

He accepted her temporary withdrawal, but suggested softly, "This could be getting serious. Maybe it's time we did something about it."

"I was thinking the same thing." Kelly couldn't resist tormenting him further. "The open house is less than a month away, and I have to plan my routine before I can practice it!"

Diego eyed her in mock annoyance, then laughed again. "You're absolutely right. How about tonight after dinner?"

"For what?"

"To work on your routine, of course." With a sly smile, he sauntered for the office door. "What did you think I meant?"

*　　*　　*

Once dinner was finished and cleared, Kelly sat down at the dining room table with some lined paper and a pencil with an eraser. Meanwhile, Diego dug through his father's collection of old, classical

LPs.

When he put one on the turntable of the stereo in the adjoining living room, Felipe hovered in fascination. "So that's how that thing works!"

"Get out of here," Diego growled at him. "You're making me feel old."

"Why are you using those...vinyl discs?"

"Records...they're called records. We're using them because Kelly had to plan out her freestyle."

"What's a freestyle?"

"It's a musical ride. And we're using these because if we played your kind of music, even Gitano would go berserk!"

Kelly, still at the table, muffled a laugh.

Felipe lingered, curious. "Can I watch you? Design the freestyle thing?"

"There's nothing to watch," Diego warned him. "You'll be bored."

Kelly explained, "I'm just drawing it, not dancing to it! That'll be Gitano's job."

They let him stay. As predicted, five minutes into the first musical passage, a march from *Aida,* Felipe lost interest and vanished.

Diego coached Kelly on the best music to use for the various gaits, and what progression would make for an interesting freestyle. Now that he'd shifted back into professional mode, Kelly was the one who found herself turned on. She grew acutely conscious of his warm presence, the always hypnotic, rolling cadence of his accent, and the breadth of his shoulders in his checked shirt. With the various crises, he hadn't made it to the barber's that month, and she relished the sexy way his black locks fringed over his collar in back.

She studied his nicely sculpted lips as he spoke, no longer hearing his words, but remembering that amazing kiss. She'd known so few men who could really kiss well! Even Neal, who thought himself so sophisticated and such a stud, used to stick his whole tongue in her mouth with no finesse whatsoever. Diego might not have played around with as many different women, but he'd learned everything he needed to know. A kiss like that promised all kinds of other talents! Just imagining what further skills Diego might posses set Kelly's nerve endings on fire all over again.

So...why had she resisted his implied invitation for tonight? She supposed because, even though they'd known each other for months, this shift in their relationship still felt sudden. Kelly suspected she was the first unattached woman with whom he'd spent very much time since his wife's death—with the possible exception of Sandy Garrett. Kelly half worried he was drawn to her chiefly out of gratitude. After all, that was what he'd said to her, just before he'd kissed her the first time. "I'm grateful…"

If his feelings went no deeper than that, maybe she shouldn't rush into anything.

Or was she over-analyzing the situation? Should she welcome his attentions on any terms? Was she still wary of being hurt again, as she had been by Neal?

"What do you think?" Diego asked, interrupting her musings.

His question yanked Kelly back to the business at hand. Because she hadn't really been paying attention for the last few minutes, it took her a moment to decipher the chart he'd drawn for her—various circles and diagonal lines within a rectangle that represented the riding arena. He explained the musical passages to be used for the different movements.

"I don't know if I'll remember all that," she told him.

"You won't, of course, until you practice it. We'll start tomorrow morning."

At that point, the phone rang, and Diego took it in the hall alcove. Kelly heard him say, in some surprise, "Oh, hello, *Don* Carlos! Yes…I guess I have some time to talk…"

At first Kelly eavesdropped, wondering if the call would shed any light on the sabotage incidents. After all, until recently Diego had suspected *Don* Carlos was the one trying to ruin him, and there was no guarantee Farley had acted alone. Working with the Villaneuvas for all those years, Farley probably would have known *Don* Carlos, or at least how to contact him.

The phone conversation wore on until Diego pulled up a side chair to listen. And, mostly, he seemed to listen. He rarely responded with anything more revealing than a "Yes, I see," and "Of course, I understand." When Kelly heard no passionate outburst, she began to doubt *Don* Carlos was either confessing to the dirty tricks or threatening more in the future.

*   *   *

Diego himself began to wonder why Salazar had taken the trouble to return his call. After all, *Don* Carlos didn't seem to have any new information to impart. No, he hadn't sent anyone to Rancho Villaneuva to buy a horse. Yes, he'd been ill with heart trouble and a few related ailments, and had scaled back lately on his own business activities.

The older man's gravelly voice did sound more halting than in the past, as if his sickness were sapping some of his legendary vitality. "When my wife told me you'd called," he said, "I started remembering the days when your family and mine used to run into each other at the Andalusian shows and breeders' functions. We had some good times back then, eh?"

"Yes," Diego agreed. Privately, he wondered if age and ill health had made *Don* Carlos forget his long feud with the Villaneuvas. Maybe standing at death's door had put it all in a different perspective for him?

"How have things been going for you, Diego? I can't be easy now that you're alone, without even your wife to help. I don't know what I'd do without my Francesca."

"I'm managing. I have a small but dedicated staff, and we're always trying to boost the business. We're even planning an open house next month."

"You don't say? That sounds like a fine idea. We used to do things like that once in a while, before my health got so bad. Do you remember the time—?" And he was off on another reminiscence.

A movement in the corner of his eye made Diego look up. Kelly had packed up her notes and was wiggling her fingers at him in a silent good-bye.

He covered the mouthpiece of the phone and asked her, "You're going?"

"It's late."

He glanced at his own watch. *Past eleven!* "It is late," he admitted. "Okay, see you tomorrow, and we'll practice."

So much, for any romantic plans he might have had in mind with Kelly. Damn, Salazar's timing was diabolical!

*   *   *

Kelly listened to the crickets throbbing and doves hooting as she made her way down the long gravel road to her bungalow. She also felt some regrets about leaving, but told herself she had nothing to lose by taking things slowly. After all, it wasn't as if she might never see Diego again. The fact that she saw him every day, even worked for him, made her extra cautious.

If they got involved briefly and then broke up, it might affect her job. Not that she thought Diego would fire her, but their situation might become too strained for her to go on working at the ranch.

Silently, she laughed at herself. *Listen to me! I've already had the affair and jumped ahead to the painful breakup! Maybe I really am a neurotic mess after all.*

She was so entangled in her thoughts that it took her a minute to notice the floodlights had come on over the front door of the main barn. The ones that responded to any movement within the radius of their sensor.

One of the barn cats passed by, she thought. *Or some stray.*

Drawing nearer, Kelly saw that the door, which they normally shut tight and latched at night, stood open a few inches.

Cold fear teased at the back of her neck, but she still rationalized the last person out of the barn must've gotten careless. Also, Helga lived in the apartment upstairs. She might have popped down to deal with something, maybe a problem with one of the horses.

Kelly nevertheless slowed and quieted her steps as she approached the open door. She thought she saw a wavering light within, as from a flashlight. Cautiously, she slid the door wider.

"Helga?" she called in a half-whisper. "Is that you? Everything all right?"

She heard a scuffling in one of the stalls about halfway down the row. At the same time the light dimmed, so she almost wondered if she'd seen it at all. Maybe it had just been the moon slanting through the skylights.

Kelly flicked on a couple of the switches that lit the barn aisle. She started to wish she had a nice, sturdy baseball bat. She considered picking up one of the manure forks, but it looked too clumsy to use as a weapon.

More shuffling and snorting. She wondered again if one of the horses were in trouble. Even in their stalls, they could get into the most amazing predicaments. They could lie down and get cast—stuck in an awkward position unable to get up—and hurt themselves badly by thrashing. And, of course, if a horse came down with colic, he might paw the floor or roll.

What if somebody was in here, and has already done something to one of them?

After a few more steps, Kelly's ears told her the restless noises came from Gitano's stall. She lost all caution then and broke into a jog. When she spotted his big, pale head through the bars, she felt some relief. At least he wasn't lying down. But his eyes showed more white

115

than normal, and he shifted in a nervous way that wasn't his usual style.

"Easy, pal," Kelly tried to soothe him. "What's the problem?"

She rolled open the door of the big box stall, just far enough to slip inside, her eyes still fastened on Gitano. She patted his neck and he quieted a bit. In the dim light of the stall, she tried to gauge his condition.

Gitano sprang back against the wall with a snort. Someone grabbed Kelly roughly from behind, pinning her arms to her sides and nearly yanking her off her feet.

A man's voice snarled in her ear, "Just be real quiet!"

CHAPTER 16

Kelly might not have recognized the voice so quickly if she hadn't been half-expecting it. She told herself Farley must have been crouching in the shadows under the feed trough.

Knowing the identity of her attacker didn't reassure her much, though. The guy had killed horses in cold blood, and she had no guarantee he would draw the line at people. She felt the prick of something sharp against her throat, which she figured was the point of a knife.

Still, she mustered the courage to demand of him, "What are you doing out here?"

"Just givin' Gitano his vitamin shot."

At first, Kelly wondered what he meant by that. She realized the point against her throat felt almost too sharp to be a knife—more like the needle of a syringe. If it were, she doubted it held anything as harmless as vitamins. At any rate, Farley still could use it to simply slash her throat.

"If you don't wanna get hurt," he growled, "better keep your mouth shut."

It was the kind of assault Kelly had feared during her years in downtown L.A., but always managed to avoid. Ironic, that she'd had to move to the country to get mugged! She knew a few self-defense tricks, but none she dared use now that Farley actually held a needle to her throat.

Kelly noticed something odd then. Although he still clutched her so tightly it hurt, Farley trembled almost as badly as she did. She guessed that, in spite of his menacing words, he hadn't the vaguest idea what to do next. He hadn't expected anyone to walk in on him tonight. She doubted he'd come prepared to kill a human being.

He still might, of course. She had no idea what was really in that syringe.

"Look," she said, "you aren't going to stab me with that thing. So far, the only crime anyone can accuse you of is trespassing. You're going to cover that up by committing murder?"

He fell silent, as if thinking. "I could bash your head in with a rock and leave you here in the stall. Everyone would think the horse did it."

In spite of her terror, Kelly had to smile. "Gitano? Yeah, he's a real killer. There's not a horse in this barn vicious enough to do a thing like that. You should know, Farley!"

She felt him flinch. "H-how do you know who I am?"

"I know you're not Eddie Hernandez. I recognized you from an old videotape. Everybody here has figured out you're the one who put oleander in the hay and set the stallion barn on fire. Of course, up to now we've had no proof."

Sensing his cowardice, Kelly grew braver. "You want my advice? Get out of here now, tonight, before you do anything else stupid. Leave California, use another fake name, and Diego will never find you. He'll have to let bygones be bygones."

Farley tensed up again. "I can't do that."

"Why not? My God, is this vendetta so important to you? So Diego told his friends you were a lousy employee. Can you blame him? In his mind, you killed his wife! You're lucky he didn't prosecute you for that. What's the point of hanging around here just to destroy his business, and getting yourself into more trouble?"

Rico's words seemed to come through gritted teeth. "Shut up! You don't understand. It's not that simple."

*   *   *

Back at the house, *Don* Carlos finally wound up his trip down memory lane.

"Well," he told Diego, "I'm probably keeping you from your rest, and I should get mine as well. I just didn't want you to think I was ignoring your call. I've done a lot of reflecting over the past few months, Diego, and I just wanted you to know—I'm not the kind of man who can go to his grave without settling things between us. You

118

understand?"

Diego wasn't sure. It was the first thing *Don* Carlos had said that sounded, very slightly, like a threat.

He was trying to decide how to reply when a buzzer sounded farther down the hall, near the front door. At first, Diego tried to account for it in some familiar way. Doorbell? Smoke alarm?

Alarm. It had to be the new one linked to the barns. He checked the panel near the near and, sure enough, found a red light blinking.

"I'm sorry, *Don* Carlos," he said into the phone. "I have to go. It could be an emergency."

*   *   *

Kelly's attempts at psychology hadn't helped her much. Farley still held her fast, with the needle tickling the flesh of her throat, and his indecision only seemed to make him more desperate. Whether or not he'd formulated a real plan, he decided to take action.

"Now," he told her, "you an' me are gonna back out of this stall, nice an' slow."

Kelly didn't mind that so much. Outside the stall, she figured she might see a better chance to break free. Anyway, Farley hadn't stabbed or slashed her with the needle yet. She told herself there had to be some reason why he was hesitating.

She shuffled sideways with Farley half dragging her. Gitano followed them out through the open door.

"Shut the stall!" Kelly told Rico, making it sound urgent. She knew he didn't really have a free hand to do it, and she hoped, in his confusion, he might drop his guard in some way.

While he paused, Diego's voice rang out sharply from the doorway of the barn. "Who's in there?"

For an instant, Rico's grip on Kelly tightened again, as if he briefly considered taking her hostage. Instead, he shoved her aside, so she landed hard on her tailbone and slammed the back of her head against the stall door. Through a haze of pain, she saw Farley grab Gitano's long mane and scramble clumsily onto the horse's bare back. She heard the clatter of hooves as he galloped Gitano down the aisle. He made for the barn door which Diego had pushed a bit wider.

Kelly couldn't tell if Diego jumped or was knocked out of the way. The gap at the door looked barely large enough for horse and rider to pass through, but Rico made it.

Diego stared after them as if tempted to give chase, but instead he jogged to Kelly's aid. "Are you hurt?"

"Not seriously. You've got to stop Farley. He'll steal Gitano!"

Diego frowned. "Bareback with no bridle? I don't think he'll hang on that long—Farley's not that good a rider. He's probably just trying to get to his truck. It's parked halfway down the drive."

Helga came running down the loft stairs in a zippered robe and bedroom slippers. "What's going on? I heard shouts, and a horse—"

Kelly explained for both of them. "Rico was hiding in Gitano's stall. When I went in there, he grabbed me, and—" Remembering the syringe, she looked around. It lay in the aisle near the open stall, and still seemed to be intact.

Just then, Gitano came trotting back into the barn, riderless, and looking bewildered by all the midnight excitement.

"I hope you broke his neck!" Kelly told the horse, putting him back in his stall.

Diego pulled his car keys from his jeans pocket. "I'm going after Farley!"

Kelly halted him with a touch on his arm. "You probably won't catch him now. You don't even know which way he's headed."

Helga agreed. "Better just to call the police. At least now we have something to accuse him of—assaulting Kelly!"

Kelly picked up the syringe and turned it over in her hand. It appeared mostly full of a thin, yellow liquid. "We may have another charge," she said, "once we get an expert to tell us what's in here."

Right after phoning the cops, Diego put in an emergency call to Dr. Newman.

*　　　*　　　*

It was past one a.m. when the vet finished examining Gitano. He told Diego and Kelly, "On just a routine check, he looks fine. No signs he's been doped or poisoned. Ms. Sheridan, did you see Farley inject the horse?"

"No. He just implied he'd already given him a shot."

Newman studied the syringe. "If the needle shows traces of hair or blood, that'll mean it penetrated the skin. Got a problem here, though—the tip's broken off."

"Probably when it fell," Diego said.

Standing in the barn aisle, Newman raised the syringe beneath the overhead, fluorescent light, and squinted at the liquid contents. "Odd…looks like some kind of serum."

"What does that mean?"

"Just that it might not be a drug as such." He dropped the thing into a clean plastic bag and sealed it up. "I'm afraid I can't tell you any more until I have my lab analyze it."

"How long will that take?"

The vet smiled sympathetically at Diego's impatience. "I'll put a rush on it. I should be able to tell you something by tomorrow afternoon."

"Thanks. I really appreciate it."

*   *   *

At Diego's insistence, both Kelly and Helga spent the rest of the night up at the main house in the two double beds in the guest room. Alonzo and Diego stayed up to keep watch over the barns, with Felipe relieving his father around dawn.

Even when his turn came to sleep, Diego remained too agitated. He pounded his pillow into a more suitable shape, imagining it was Farley's face.

He wished he'd acted more quickly the night before, and yanked that little *bastardo* off the horse. But it all had happened too fast. In the dark, he hadn't even realized the rider was Farley until the guy had galloped past him. And then it had been more important to see if Kelly was okay. Luckily, except for a few bruises, she was.

Just remembering it all, Diego ground his molars in fury. This had gone way past sabotaging his business or even harming his horses. Rico had cost him Isabella, and last night he could very well have hurt or even killed Kelly. Diego didn't want to think what could have happened to her if he hadn't come into the barn when he had.

Even if the police eventually caught Farley, jail wasn't bad enough for him. *At this point,* thought Diego, *he'd better hope the cops get to him before I do!*

*   *   *

Late that afternoon, Kelly was returning from the tack room and passing the barn office when she heard Diego's voice through the open door. He sounded as if he were on the phone, his long pauses punctuated with only a few subdued questions.

"Isn't there anything else we can do?" he asked. Then, "When will we know for sure?"

Finally he thanked someone in a dull voice, and she heard him drop the phone back into its cradle. Kelly peered around the doorjamb and saw him slumped in his desk chair with a dazed expression. It turned to outright pain when he met her eyes.

"What's wrong?"

"That was Dr. Newman. He says the stuff in the syringe was a virus—equine infectious anemia. More commonly known as swamp fever. Ever hear of it?"

She nodded. "Isn't that the disease they screen for with the Coggins test? That can disqualify a horse from showing?"

Diego nodded. "For good reason, too. He says it's highly contagious among horses, and incurable. If Gitano has been exposed to it, we may have to destroy not only him, but every horse on my property!"

CHAPTER 17

Kelly groped for a seat on the office's ombre-striped sofa. "Diego, that can't be true!"

"I'm afraid it is. If Farley accomplished his purpose last night, then he's won. I'm wiped out."

"How…how long until you know for sure?"

Diego sighed deeply. "Newman can do blood tests on Gitano, and the other horses in the main barn. Any horse that has been exposed to the virus will show antibodies in his blood in about thirty days. Lord, that means we won't know for a month!"

"And if they do show antibodies?"

"They have to be put down, or else kept in quarantine for the rest of their lives—which would destroy my business, anyway. And every horse in the barn would have to be considered exposed. The virus is spread by flies and we have our share around here. We might save the young horses kept out in the pastures, but even that would be a long shot."

Kelly could think of nothing more to say just then. She crossed to Diego and put her arms around him. The way his hand gripped hers in return told her he appreciated the support.

"At least this stuff is harmless to people," he told her. "Even if that *bastardo* had stuck you with the needle, it wouldn't have made you sick."

"It's going to be all right," Kelly promised him, while fighting down the lump in her throat. "You won't lose the ranch. I'll bet we won't even lose Gitano. Can we move him away from the other horses until we find out if he's sick or not?"

"It doesn't guarantee anything, but we can try." Diego gave her an apologetic half-smile. "One thing's for sure—the open house is off. We'll have to quarantine the whole place and that's not going to make it very attractive to visitors." A sudden thought made him grimace in further anguish. "Oh God, wait 'til Mrs. Konrad hears about this."

*   *   *

Their boarder reacted just as badly as Diego had feared. Furious over the threat to her horse, she didn't seem to care that Diego was not responsible for this new crisis. She vowed that if Redwood came down with the virus and had to be destroyed, she would sue Diego for everything he had. He could only reply, miserably, that she might as well because by that time he wouldn't have much.

Dr. Newman came the next day to draw the first blood sample from Gitano, who endured the annoyance with his typical stoicism. Diego and Kelly stood by during the procedure, to ask the vet more questions about the illness.

"First, I'm going to do a C-ELISA test," Newman told them. "It's faster than the Coggins test, and if he's negative on that, it may put your minds at ease a little bit. But it's not as accurate as the Coggins, so you should still wait for those results before you lift the quarantine."

Kelly shrugged. "Even if we have to scrap the open house, the main thing is finding out if the horses can be saved."

Newman nodded. "Y'know, even if you two hadn't seen Farley with the hypo, and the horses had just come down with the virus, it still would've looked suspicious. Equine infectious anemia isn't really common anymore, especially not in this part of the country. They call it swamp fever because you mostly see it in marshy places where there are lots of mosquitoes and flies."

Diego found this interesting, but not especially helpful. "I guess Farley wasn't too concerned about whether or not it would look suspicious. He wanted a disease that would spread through my whole stock and wipe me out. Sounds like he picked the right one."

Kelly asked the vet, "If the virus is so rare around here, though, where could Farley have gotten it?"

"Good question. Maybe from a research facility or a veterinary school." Newman started packing up his medical kit. "Even if he had access to an infected animal...from what you say about him, I doubt he made the serum himself! That stuff had to have come from a professional lab."

*   *   *

They moved Gitano to a pasture at a distance from the other horses and disinfected his stall. They kept his brushes, buckets or other equipment away from those used for the other animals. As Diego had said, this didn't guarantee the virus would not, or had not, spread around the barn. In the time it had taken them to get the vet's report, Gitano had remained in his usual stall, and there was a slim chance he'd been bitten by a fly or two. Since he showed no signs yet of lethargy, fever or lack of appetite, though, they could hope at least he wasn't contagious.

Because Gitano now had to be turned out all day and all night, Kelly decided to get him a fly sheet—a lightweight, mesh covering that would keep insects from biting his shoulders, back and flanks. She felt like giving him something to make up for all the trouble he'd endured, and might still have to endure. She planned to spend her own money, and didn't want Diego to talk her out of it, so she left while he was still finishing up with Newman.

During her drive, she considered what the vet had said about the swamp fever serum. If the virus was rare in that part of the country and the serum had to be processed by a lab, then it did seem beyond Farley's skills to concoct such a scheme.

Did he have an accomplice?

She remembered what he'd said when she was trying to persuade him to give up his vendetta and just leave town. "You don't understand. It's not that simple."

Of course. Farley wasn't acting out of just his own personal malice. Even he wasn't that stupid. Someone had put him up to this. Someone with money, a knowledge of horses and ranches, and an interest in ruining Diego.

That put two prime suspects back into the picture—*Don* Carlos and Sandy Garrett.

*   *   *

At Aiken's Feed, Kelly found a fly sheet in the right size at a reasonable price. She would have felt happier about buying Gitano a present if she knew for sure he would live long enough to enjoy it. The rage she felt towards Farley now expanded to include whoever had been cruel enough to hire him for such a stunt.

Driving back to the ranch, Kelly remained so intent on solving the puzzle that it took her a while to really notice the vehicle jouncing along in front of her.

An old red Ford pickup with a gray left door on the cab.

The driver wore some kind of cap, so she guessed it to be a man, but otherwise she couldn't identify him. She memorized the license plate, then eased back so he wouldn't realize she was following.

When the turn came that would have taken her towards Rancho Villanueva, she passed it and kept going.

Am I crazy? she asked herself. *Even if it is Farley, why am I tailing him? Do I think I can get out and throttle him with my bare hands?* Furious as she was, she would have liked to try. But then she recalled the way he'd easily pinned her arms while holding the syringe to her throat. He wasn't big, but he was pretty strong. More likely he'd end up throttling her.

She wished she had a car phone to call the police and report she'd spotted him. The only thing she really could do, she decided, was find out where he was headed.

She even let another car get in between them for a while because the road was so straight she could still easily keep the red truck in her sights. All at once, he turned off down a gravel side street marked La Jolla Drive.

It became harder for Kelly to remain inconspicuous then, with no other cars on the road, and she dropped back a little farther. She saw several low, butter-yellow buildings up ahead on the left with paddocks fenced in sparkling white, and realized it must be a horse ranch. A well-kept one, too. Had somebody hired Farley after all, despite his blackened reputation?

The red truck veered down a short, private drive and parked near a small, aluminum-sided house that looked like the equivalent of Kelly's own bungalow—an employee's residence. She pulled over to the side of the road and waited long enough to see the driver get out. She was still pretty far away, but from his walk, it did look like Farley.

She knew she couldn't stay around unless she wanted to force a one-on-one confrontation. And that seemed pointless when there were more effective things she could do.

She K-turned the Blazer and headed back to Rancho Villaneuva.

*   *   *

126

She found Diego in the stable yard with Helga, probably bringing her up to date on what the vet had said. Breathlessly, Kelly told them she thought she'd spotted Farley, and reeled off the license number of the truck.

Diego's deep frown told her it was a match, even before he explained, "The HRL on the plate—we used to joke behind Farley's back that it stood for 'His Royal Laziness.'"

"It turned down La Jolla Road and parked near a bungalow," Kelly told them. "He could be living there! Do you have any idea who owns that property?"

Diego looked stricken and didn't answer right away.

Helga couldn't help prompting him. "Isn't that..."

Avoiding their eyes, he answered in a low, taut voice. "It's Sandy Garrett's place."

Kelly knew it pained him to think Sandy might be harboring his worst enemy. Still, this was their chance to nab Farley, and they shouldn't blow it. "We have to tell the police!"

Diego pivoted towards the barn. "First, I have to call Sandy."

No! Kelly shouted inside. *If she hired Farley, she'll tip him off! He'll disappear, and she'll just cover her tracks!* More tactfully, she asked, "Do you think that's wise? I mean—"

"She may not know anything about Farley being on her property. Maybe he's planning on sabotaging her, too."

As he left for the barn office, Kelly and Helga watched in dismay.

"I didn't realize he felt so...loyal towards her," said Kelly.

"He could be right," Helga ventured, though she sounded skeptical.

"Or Sandy could be behind everything that's been going wrong around here! Maybe she really, really wants Diego to merge his ranch with hers—among other things—and she's trying to make it impossible for him to survive on his own."

Helga's blue eyes looked pained. "It's hard to believe she would be that cruel."

"I know. But she sure acted jealous when she saw me with him at the fundraiser...and almost disappointed when he said his business was turning around. Lust can make people do crazy things." Kelly still wouldn't mention her theory about the crushed hat in the *arroyo,* and Isabella's suspicious accident.

To change the subject, Kelly showed Helga the gift she'd bought for Gitano. They discussed all the precautions they were going to have to take to keep him from potentially infecting the other horses.

Finally, Diego emerged from the barn, his stride defiant. When he reached the two women, he spoke firmly. "Just as I supposed—Sandy says she had no idea Farley was on her property. She's very upset about it. She's going right out to that bungalow to see if he's still there."

Helga gave him a crooked smile. "Armed, I hoped!"

Kelly flapped her arms in exasperation. "Diego, you should've called the cops first. Now Farley will take off and we'll never seen him again."

"Sandy's going to call the police."

"Are you sure?" Kelly decided honesty might be more important, at this point, than kindness. "What if she put Farley up to all this?" When Diego looked shocked, Kelly explained why she thought the ex-groom must've had a well-to-do, knowledgeable accomplice.

Even Helga had to admit, "Kelly's right. The poisoning and the fire, he could have done alone. But this business with the virus..."

Diego's eyes flashed with the kind of temper Kelly hadn't seen since those first, moody days of their early acquaintance. "Sandy is a friend. She may be a little spoiled and selfish, but she wouldn't try to destroy my ranch. I won't listen to any more of this!" Waving an arm as if to physically ward off their words, he stalked away towards the stallion barn.

Helga only sighed. "I hope he's right. Don't you?"

*　　*　　*

The argument left things strained between Kelly and Diego for the next few days. They spoke about routine matters and ways of coping with the latest crisis, but not as intimately or warmly as before.

True to Kelly's prediction, Farley had disappeared from the Lucky Shot by the time Sandy went out to check for him. Or, at least, that's what Sandy told Diego.

Gavin Thorne, back from his travels, finally returned Diego's call. He said he didn't remember seeing anyone who fit Farley's description, but admitted so many people passed through the resort he might not have noticed. He promised to have his employees keep an eye out for anyone who wasn't a paying guest, and seemed to be acting suspiciously. Diego supposed that was all the man could do.

With the open house indefinitely postponed, Diego spent less time training the horses. Kelly thought it was almost as if he'd given up and resigned himself once again to losing the ranch. Instead, he took long rides on Hidalgo, alone. He never asked Kelly to go with him, and she didn't offer.

He wouldn't want me to ride Gitano, anyway, would he? she reminded herself. *Gitano is a pariah now—he might infect Hidalgo.*

Kelly stopped riding the freckled gelding completely, concerned that hard work might wear down his resistance to the virus. Sometimes he seemed to enjoy being turned out, and cantered like a colt around his private field. At other times, though, Kelly found him with his head over the fence, staring down towards the main barn and neighing pathetically to his distant equine friends. Whenever he appeared even slightly listless, drowsy or off his feed, she worried the disease might finally be taking a hold on him.

One afternoon she broke down, threw her arms around his burly neck and sobbed into his long, silky, bronze mane, wondering how everything had suddenly gone so far off track. A week ago, she and Diego had been growing closer, the ranch had been gaining ground financially, and they'd been planning a terrific open house. Now it was all shot to hell. By that little piece of scum, Rico Farley.

No, Kelly thought. *Not by Rico alone. It couldn't have been. But if Sandy did put Rico up to it, Diego will never believe it.*

Kelly felt a hand on her shoulder and jumped. Diego had joined her, his steps muffled by the paddock's grass. His expression looked softer than it had in days, maybe because he'd seen her crying. There was something else, too. He looked almost… cheerful.

"We may be able to stop mourning him," Diego said, with a glance at Gitano. "He may be sticking around for a while after all."

Kelly's heart bounded with hope. "What do you mean?"

"Dr. Newman called. The second round of Coggins tests on Gitano and the other horses in the main barn came back negative, just like the first. We'll do a third round just to be sure, but it's a good sign. Newman says most likely they were never even exposed to the virus."

"Then…Farley never injected Gitano?"

"Sounds like you may have interrupted him just in time." Diego slapped the horse's neck and told him, "You owe this young lady your life, *amigo*. Better treat her good from now on!"

"He always does." Kelly started crying again, this time from happiness. "I'm so relieved! I'm sure you are, too."

"Relieved doesn't describe it—I'm almost shocked! I was sure Farley had really done it this time, and I was finished." He wrapped an arm around Kelly's shoulders. "Let's go back to the house and tell the Martinezes. I don't think it's too early to celebrate over dinner tonight."

On their stroll down the dirt road to the barn, Kelly felt as if things were falling back into place after all. Her elation was cut short, though, by the sight of two patrol cars parked in the barnyard, and a pair of officers talking to Helga.

When she saw Kelly and Diego approaching, Helga paled. A sturdy, blond policeman stepped forward and asked, "You Diego Villaneuva?"

He nodded, his eyes curious.

"I'm going to have to ask you to come down to the station with us and answer a few questions."

"What's this about?" Diego demanded.

The cop jerked his head in the direction of the back fifteen. "We found a body on your property this afternoon with his skull bashed in." He flipped open a tooled black wallet to double check the I.D. "Guy by the name of Rico Farley."

CHAPTER 18

Seated across the desk from Sheriff Michaels at the police station, Diego soon understood he was the chief suspect in Rico Farley's apparent murder.

"Mr. Villaneuva, you filed a complaint against Mr. Farley about a week ago, didn't you? Something about his trespassing on your property and doing some damage?"

"He tried to kill one of my horses, and threatened...an employee." Diego went on to explain what they'd discovered about the serum in the syringe.

Michaels looked grave. "Serious stuff. He could've destroyed your business. What reason would he have for doing something like that?"

"I really don't know, except that I fired him a year ago. For...negligence."

"What kind of negligence?"

Diego hesitated. "He made a mistake that caused a serious accident."

The sheriff pinned him with an unwavering look. "This is a small town, Mr. Villaneuva. I already know you blame Farley for the death of your wife."

Diego couldn't hold back a sour smile. "If I were going to kill him for that, I would have done it a year ago. I wouldn't have waited this long!"

"Depends. Maybe you lost track of him for a while. Then he shows up again, and now he's trying to kill off your stock and ruin your business. That might've finally pushed you over the edge."

"He escaped from my barn a week ago, and I never saw him again…until just now when you showed me his body."

The sheriff nodded, although Diego couldn't tell if he really bought the explanation, and made some notes. "Mr. Villaneuva, where were you yesterday between two and six p.m.?"

"Two and six?" He tried to remember. "Between about two and four, I went out riding. After that, I made the rounds with Dr. Newman, while he took blood from my horses."

"You went riding alone? On your back property?"

"Yes."

"What horse did you use?"

Diego found this an odd question, but answered willingly. "My younger stallion, Hidalgo."

"You didn't see anything or anyone suspicious while you were out there?"

"No."

"Because judging from the condition of the body, Farley was killed yesterday afternoon between two and six. He was found not far from that deep *arroyo* on your property. There were no tire tracks anywhere around—only hoofprints."

Diego shuddered to imagine someone on horseback dumping a body on his land without his knowing anything about it. From what he'd seen of the corpse, Rico had died of a crushed skull that left him barely recognizable. "Did you find a weapon?"

"No…but you might not have needed one. Not if you were riding this fellow."

The sheriff slid forward, across his blotter, a clipping of the *Sun* article. The photo showed Hidalgo suspended in mid-air doing his best *capriole,* with his hind legs outstretched in a powerful kick.

Diego felt dizzy with fear and confusion. They thought he'd used Hidalgo to kill Rico! "That's crazy! Do you think I went riding and just happened to run into Farley?"

"Maybe you arranged to meet him."

"Hah! Even Farley wouldn't be stupid enough to meet me in such a lonely spot when he knows how much I hate him."

"Maybe he contacted you to make some kind of deal, and you pretended to agree, so you could get the drop on him."

Diego raked his hand back through his hair in frustration. "Okay, tell me—how did I get him to stand still, in just the right spot, so

Hidalgo could kick him?"

"I don't know, Mr. Villaneuva. You're the horse trainer, not me."

Diego realized they could easily hold him for murder. He appeared to have both the motive and the opportunity, at least from the sheriff's viewpoint. "I'm curious about something. With all that empty land, can you tell me how you found Rico's body? And so quickly?"

The sheriff almost smiled, as if Diego were finally admitting they'd outsmarted him. "Guy in a helicopter spotted it. The pilot who flies that golden chopper for Rio Dorado."

Diego nodded, considering this. "Okay. If I killed this guy on my own land, in a lonely spot with no witnesses, and I know Thorne's helicopter flies over now and then...why would I leave the body out in the open? Why wouldn't I bury it or at least hide it? Why would anybody leave it in plain sight?"

Diego could see he finally had Michaels stumped.

"Good question. You tell me."

"Because somebody is trying to frame me. The same person who has been trying to drive me out of business. Obviously Farley was a...a pawn for someone else, someone who got tired of him messing up. This is just one last attempt to ruin me."

The sheriff finally looked as if he were coming around to Diego's side. "I guess that could be."

Feeling more confident now, Diego pressed on. "It's true that I hated Farley. But I'd already figured out he probably wasn't working alone." He explained why the virus plot seemed beyond Rico's limited capabilities. "So why would I kill him? I wanted him arrested, so he could tell us who hired him!"

Although the sheriff frowned, it was a compliant, you-got-me-there expression. "I see your point, Mr. Villaneuva. And since we don't have any witnesses or a murder weapon, I'll let you go for now. After we get the coroner's report, though, we may be back in touch."

Relieved, Diego got to his feet, his knees still a bit shaky. "My bet is Farley was killed some other way, and they bashed in his head to cover it up. Tell the coroner to check for a bullet wound."

The uniformed man regarded Diego with new respect. "We'll do that."

*   *   *

Back at the main house at Rancho Villaneuva, Kelly and Helga sat on the living room sofa and fretted.

After a silence, Kelly asked, "You don't think Diego did kill Farley? Could he have run into Rico out there and just...lost it?"

Helga's eyes focused in that quick, angry way that always came as a surprise. "No. Nothing would make him do that. He has too much self-respect."

Kelly nodded, glad to have her own faith re-affirmed. "I wish I'd gone down to the station with him, but I didn't want to look like I was...y'know, interfering."

Helga grunted in agreement.

When the hall phone rang, Kelly jumped for it. But it was only Sandy Garrett, looking for Diego. Even though she still didn't trust Sandy, Kelly felt she had to explain what had happened.

"They found Farley dead? Oh, my God! And they're blaming Diego? What can I do? Does he need someone to post bail?"

Sandy and her money to the rescue, Kelly thought. "I don't know if he's been arrested yet. They're just questioning him."

A groan on the line. "I wish I could help. I called because I found out why Farley was at my place yesterday."

"Oh?" Kelly looked forward to this explanation.

"He was having a fling with my maid, Carla. I didn't know anything about it. I feel so stupid! She has her own bungalow—that's where you saw him park. It's out of sight of my house, and I don't keep close tabs on her social life."

"No, of course not."

"He did tell Carla he got a job doing errands for somebody important, and that's why he suddenly had money. Unfortunately, he was smart enough not to tell her who hired him. If her testimony will help Diego, though, I'll trot her little butt down to the police station, right now!"

Before Kelly could reply, the front door flew open and Diego paced in. Relief washed over Kelly in a flood. "I don't think that'll be necessary, Sandy. He's already back."

Diego glanced from Kelly to the phone. "Is that Garrett? Let me talk to her."

Kelly handed over the headset, disappointed. She wanted to throw her arms around him, tell him how worried she'd been, and ask him how he'd managed to get free. It didn't seem fair that the first person to welcome him back should be Sandy.

He spent a few minutes on the phone explaining things, including how he'd convinced the police of his probable innocence. "So for now, anyway, I don't need bail. But you can do something else for me. Your offer to keep my stallions at your place—does that still stand?" He listened for a beat. "Good. I'll send them over tonight. Thanks a lot."

Kelly's heart froze. *Don't do it!* she wanted to scream. *If Sandy's behind all this, you'll be playing right into her hands!*

Hanging up, Diego turned to see Kelly's reproachful stare. His response was defensive. "Don't start that again! I trust Sandy. But whoever hired Rico is still out there. Just because Rico's dead doesn't mean the threat is over."

"No, it certainly doesn't," said Helga, joining them. "At least Farley seemed reluctant to kill a human being. His boss doesn't have the same scruples."

With a glance that swept over the house, Diego frowned. "Now I'm worried about somebody breaking in here and hurting one of you. I wish I could post a real, armed guard. Sandy's got a lot of hands over at her ranch...I wonder if she'd lend us one of them."

Kelly laid a hand on his arm. "Diego, before you go any further with this, I have something I want to show you. It's down in my bungalow."

*   *   *

She took the half-crushed, pearl-gray hat from its nail, handed it to him and explained where she'd found it.

Diego turned it over in his square, strong hands, examining the fine materials and Stetson label. "Why didn't you show this to me sooner?"

"I didn't know if it meant anything, and I didn't want to remind you unnecessarily of...the accident. After we found out Eddie and Rico were one and the same, I thought it probably belonged to him. I have to admit, though, it gave me another reason to suspect Sandy."

His eyes and tone sharpened again. "Why?"

"When we saw her at the fundraiser, she was wearing a white hat a lot like this. I mean, riding and shooting in all those Western events and dressing like Annie Oakley half the time, she probably has a whole wardrobe of the things! Diego, if it is hers, it means at least she was on your property without you knowing about it."

He tossed the hat onto Kelly's tweed sofa. "Even that wouldn't make her guilty of anything. And it's still a big 'if.' I think your first guess was right—it belonged to Farley. Probably just one of the luxuries he bought with the pay he collected for poisoning my mares."

Kelly knew she'd hit a stone wall. "I just thought you should see it before you shipped your stallions over to Sandy's ranch."

The creases in his forehead deepened, and his answer dripped sarcasm. "Thank you for your concern, but my horses will be perfectly safe at Sandy's. Probably a lot safer than—"

He broke off when his new cell phone rang. He tugged it from his back pocket and lost a few seconds figuring out how to answer it.

His half of the conversation was so monosyllabic that Kelly didn't learn much from it, until the end. Then he said, almost cheerfully, "I promise you, sheriff, you can search my property from end to end and you won't find any guns. I've never owned one in my life, and I'm sure the same goes for my employees."

After a moment, Diego added, "That reminds me—if I'm no longer under suspicion, would it be possible to post one of your men out here, at least for the next couple of nights? After all, someone was killed on my land and the killer could come back." From Diego's half-smile and gracious thanks, Kelly knew the sheriff had agreed.

After he hung up, he told her, "I was right. Farley didn't die from the crushed skull—first he was shot. The coroner couldn't tell anything more, except it was at pretty close range. The bullet went right through."

"It's a good thing you never bought a gun," Kelly said.

"It is. And with any luck, I won't have to. Michaels said he'll be sending a cruiser by the ranch, at least for the next couple of nights."

"That should help."

Diego seemed to dismiss their previous argument. "Well, I'm going to have some supper, and after that I'll trailer those horses over to the Lucky Shot."

Where, Kelly thought, *they have plenty of guns.*

CHAPTER 19

Over the next few days, the atmosphere at the ranch felt oppressive to Kelly. All of them seemed to be looking over their shoulders, waiting for the next blow to fall.

The horses were finally declared disease-free, and the man who'd seemed their greatest threat no longer existed, but still no one could breathe easy. The unknown mastermind behind the sabotage remained at large, and there was no guarantee he'd given up his plan to destroy Rancho Villaneuva.

Or she. Kelly still didn't completely trust Sandy Garrett. She figured Diego sensed this because his behavior towards Kelly remained cool. If only for the sake of their relationship, she hoped she was wrong about Sandy.

Lunging Redwood one morning, Kelly again mentally flipped through the clues to determine who else might be a likely suspect.

The oleander and the matchbook both had come from Rio Dorado, which could implicate Gavin Thorne. Still, Rico could've obtained those materials from the resort, no matter for whom he was working.

Thorne's helicopter pilot had reported seeing Rico's body. Was that just a coincidence?

On the other hand, either Sandy or *Don* Carlos would've been more likely to think of the oleander and the swamp fever virus to disable Diego's horses. Being in the same business, either might've known of a lab that would make up the serum.

A crooked vet? Kelly wondered. *He'd have to have a pretty big,*

137

sophisticated lab. Otherwise, it could've been done at a veterinary college or an agricultural school—

She stiffened so abruptly that Redwood felt the tug on the lunge line, and lapsed from his trot into a walk.

At the fundraiser, didn't Thorne say he went to an agricultural school?

It should be possible to find out more about that.

Kelly gave Mrs. Konrad's horse five more preoccupied minutes, cooled him out, then brushed him and put him away. She slipped into the barn office and phoned Judy at work.

"Can you do me a favor? Wally represents Gavin Thorne's resorts. Would you have access to any background material on Thorne himself?"

"Gee, I dunno," said Judy. "Nothing very confidential. Wally would keep that in his private files."

"I don't necessarily need any big secrets. I'm just looking for some insight into what kind of guy he is, how he operates...and especially where he grew up and went to school."

"I can try," Judy said.

"I'd be grateful. I know you're busy, but the sooner you can get it to me, the better." Kelly gave her friend both the ranch's e-mail address and the number for the office fax machine.

She spent the next hour working with Belleza, who fortunately was on her good behavior that day. By the time Kelly dropped by the office again, saw she a fresh fax in the tray of the machine. It was a profile done on Thorne the previous fall in a national business magazine. On the cover sheet, Judy had scrawled, *This was all I could find without making Wally too suspicious of my motives. Hope it tells you what you need to know!*

The author of the article seemed to admire Thorne's drive while reserving judgment on his character. He included one particularly colorful insight:

"Growing up the eldest of seven children in rural Missouri, Thorne had to fight hard for everything he got, including an education. While most successful entrepreneurs can point to their Harvard MBAs, he has never concealed the fact that his only degree comes from Asheville College, a small agricultural school in the Missouri backwaters; these days, his generous endowments may be all that keeps the school going.

"The new, improved Thorne speaks with barely a trace of a drawl, and dresses out of Brooks Brothers. When the chips are down, though, he quickly reverts to his roots as a backwoods scrapper, who considers no holds barred."

*   *   *

At the main house, just before lunch, Kelly showed Diego a printout of the item. "Asheville College in Missouri! Sounds to me like just the place to have a little equine infectious anemia virus sitting around in the refrigerator!"

Diego studied the printout with a grave expression. "Missouri's a long way to go for it, but…I suppose it's possible."

"If he's the school's biggest donor, I'm sure he could lean on someone in the lab to make up any vile concoction he wanted, ship it to him and not ask any questions." Kelly felt triumphant. "Now all we have to do it get good ol' Sheriff Michaels to call the cops in Asheville and ask them to check it out."

Diego's eyebrows lowered. "Do you really think it'll be that easy? I'm going to accuse the great Gavin Thorne of thinking up dirty tricks to drive me out of business! It sounds so absurd. Why would he bother?"

"Maybe he really, really wants your land."

Diego appeared to consider this. "Last year, about a month after Isabella died, Thorne invited me over to meet with him at the resort. He asked me then if I was interested in selling this place, and made me a generous offer. I was still so upset about Isabella that I didn't want to even think about such a thing. I told him I'd never consider selling, that I felt I owed it to the memories of my wife and my father to keep the ranch going and make it succeed."

All of this made sense to Kelly. "So you left Thorne with the impression nothing would ever change your mind…unless your business foundered so badly you had no other choice!"

"I see what you mean." With a shake of his head, Diego crossed to the front hall telephone. "I'll try to convince Michaels. I just hope he doesn't slam the phone down too hard in my ear."

Kelly followed and gave him a teasing elbow in the ribs. "Hey, aren't you proud of me?"

"For remembering what Thorne said about having gone to an agricultural school? Yeah, that was pretty good."

"Not just that. I'm finally suspicious of somebody besides Sandy Garrett!"

*   *   *

Unfortunately, Michaels reacted to the call almost as badly as Diego had predicted. He listened politely, but sounded skeptical that a man of Thorne's stature would deal with someone like Rico Farley and stoop to undermining Diego. The sheriff did promise to look into the connection with Asheville College, but didn't sound as if he planned to expend too much energy on the project.

Diego hung up with a hollow feeling in his gut. "There could be something to your theory, Kelly, but I don't know how we're going to prove it."

She sank onto the living room's Mission sofa, her hands clasped between her knees and her elfin features bowed in concentration. "There must be something else we can do. It feels terrible to just sit around here so…passively."

Diego slumped with his shoulder blades against the hall doorjamb. "It may be time to give up the fight anyway. Farley may be gone, but whoever hired him may have accomplished his goal. This place is seriously in debt, and I don't see much chance of digging myself back out again."

Kelly looked shocked, then thoughtful. "Wow! I guess with rebuilding the barn, and putting in the new security systems, and then the blood tests on all the horses…"

"My insurance covered some of it, but not enough. And the last time I tried for a bank loan, remember, they turned me down." Diego hesitated to bring up one possible solution because he knew how Kelly would react to it. He laughed, to make it sound like a joke. "Sandy offered to lend me the money, interest free. I'd almost take her up on it, if I could see any hope of repaying her."

Kelly's eyes narrowed into lethal daggers. "Interest free—I'll bet! And I'm sure she'd think of a way you could repay her!"

Although he knew Kelly was probably right, Diego slapped the oak doorjamb in exasperation. "Well, what else can I do? I can't even afford to go back to Spain unless I sell out to Thorne, and just in case you're right about him, I'll be damned before I'll do that."

Kelly met his gaze, cool as a cat. "How much do we really need? To keep going for, say, three or four more months?" Even when he told her, she didn't flinch. "Maybe we could make that much. How about going back to the idea of an open house? We can use it as a fundraiser and charge admission."

This struck him as tacky. "I don't know—make people pay to come to our ranch? Who would do that?"

"Don't forget, we're going to give them a good show. A lot of people have never seen horses as talented as yours. Heck, they charge people plenty to see the Lipizzaners. Why shouldn't they pay a couple of bucks to watch Gitano and Hidalgo?"

Diego considered this. Even if charging admission felt awfully...undignified, he supposed it would be better than taking a handout from Sandy Garrett.

"Maybe we could sell some food, too," Kelly went on, her event-planning skills obviously in high gear. "We'll have to keep the prices down, of course. We'll just hope enough people show up to put us back in the black."

"What about safety?" Diego reminded her. "After all that's gone on, do we dare let a bunch of strangers in here?"

"I'll bet we could get Sheriff Michaels to help us with that—to send over a couple of his guys for the day." Kelly's eyes twinkled shrewdly. "Maybe it wouldn't be such a bad thing if our enemy did show up. He might do something to tip his hand."

It sounded risky to Diego, but better than taking no action at all. He agreed with Kelly that it was torture to just sit around in limbo. And if he didn't do something, his unknown tormentor would win. A glance at the mantel clock told him Helga, Alonzo and Felipe would soon be arriving for lunch.

"Okay," he relented. "Let's tell everybody the show's back on!"

*   *   *

At first, Kelly was delighted Diego had agreed to resume plans for the open house. She soon discovered, though, that there was a down side.

Now that the stallions had gone to Sandy's ranch, if Diego wanted to practice on Hidalgo, he had to do it over there. So did Felipe, when Diego coached him at jumping Basilio. Not only did Kelly see far less of Diego than usual, she had to wonder how much he was seeing of Sandy.

Because she knew that would be a sore subject, she complained only generally about missing him. She did so one afternoon as he was about to step into his Range Rover and take off for the Lucky Shot. His face folded in what looked like genuine regret and he put his arms around her in a gentle embrace.

"I'm sorry I have to be away so much," he said, "but Hidalgo needs the practice. I haven't been able to ride him much for the last couple of months, between hurting my ribs and then that virus scare. He needs to sharpen up."

Kelly played the guilt card. "I thought you were going to help me with my routine."

"I know, and I will. But I also have to work with Felipe." Diego smiled sheepishly. "If he falls off Basilio, and gets hurt, Nora will kill me! At least I know you'll be safe on Gitano. I'll work with you soon, I promise." After giving her a warm, but brief kiss, he drove away.

Kelly watched him go with a childish disappointment gnawing at her insides. It triggered memories of her father's mysterious, increasing absences once he began sleeping with his hygienist. Until then, he used to come home promptly for dinner during the week, and at noon on Saturdays. Suddenly he had more emergencies and paperwork to keep him working late at his dental office.

Kelly supposed she could trust Diego while Felipe was along. But Felipe only practiced for a couple of hours in the morning, then came back to finish his chores. Diego spent plenty of time at the Lucky Shot on his own with only Hidalgo for a chaperone.

At the end of the first week, he called Nora in the early evening to say he wouldn't be back for supper. Sandy had invited him to dine with her.

"And her guys, he says." Nora relayed the message to the rest of them with a mischievous glint in her eye. "As if they're going to eat with the ranch hands!"

Alonzo shrugged. "We all eat together here."

"There ain't many of us. Sandy Garrett's got a dozen hired hands. Me, I think they eat in a kitchen, and she eat somewhere else."

Alonzo kept a straight face, made especially droll by his floppy moustache. "If she does, she must get very lonely."

Helga sniffed. "No wonder she wants company for dinner!"

Kelly said nothing, and the others didn't seem to notice her fuming. None of them really knew about her feelings for Diego—feelings she'd thought he reciprocated. Helga had been nudging them together, true, but even she wasn't aware how successful her efforts had been.

At least, Kelly thought, *until now.*

Maybe she'd made a mistake by accusing Sandy of the sabotage. Diego had felt obliged to defend his neighbor, and maybe that had softened his feelings towards her. Had he come to see Kelly as the ogre, unfairly attacking poor, innocent Sandy? That seemed preposterous, but Kelly knew men certainly could be fooled that way. Look how her father had fallen for that manipulative girl in her twenties, thinking of her as sweet and helpless. He talked about how much she needed him, while his wife was facing down cancer!

The ache settled as a weight in Kelly's chest. She'd imagined Diego as a person of real conviction, who would dedicate himself to an ideal and never falter. Now she saw he was as shallow and easily swayed as any other man. For a second, Kelly considered throwing herself at him to distract him from Sandy, but she had too much pride. Then she decided she was glad she'd never actually slept with him because she would feel less attached if he let her down now.

She remember something Helga had said once—that maybe if Diego could blame someone besides himself for Isabella's death, he would feel free to love another woman. Perhaps something like that had happened after he'd confronted Rico once more. Maybe Diego felt free to give his heart again.

Only instead of her, he'd chosen Sandy.

CHAPTER 20

The outdoor ring at Rancho Villaneuva had speakers on poles at either end, wired up to an old tape deck in the barn office. Diego had made tapes of his classical records, and Kelly tried to practice the freestyle routine he'd designed for her. Without him around to encourage her, however, she found her heart wasn't really in it.

For one thing, although she knew most dressage riders performed to classical music, it wasn't her personal taste. Riding Gitano to stately marches felt, to her, a bit too Old World. It might work if she were performing before European judges, but she worried it would turn off the kind of casual audience likely to show up for the open house.

One morning, as Kelly was tacking up with a tape of her own playing on a nearby boom box, she found herself listening to it with a fresh ear. In the soft-rock recording, she heard a beat that sounded like a good match for Gitano's trot. Halfway through came a shift that might work with his canter…then the trot rhythm again.

Fired with new inspiration, Kelly rewound the tape, popped it out and brought it to the office. She let it run through a few earlier songs while she brought her horse outside, mounted and warmed up. By the time it reached the number she wanted, she had Gitano moving out at a brisk, smooth pace.

The speakers, though fuzzy with age, blared a crisp drumbeat, throbbing bass, bouncy lead guitar and upbeat vocals. Gitano fell right into the groove, and suddenly Kelly started having fun again. She experimented at the trot with his half-pass, shoulder-in and haunches-in, and really felt as if they were dancing. When the switch came to the rolling canter rhythm, she signaled him and he took off crisply, doing some of the same moves, plus a half-pirouette and a few flying changes.

Kelly heard the end of the song coming and steered Gitano down the center line, where she tried the *passage*-into-*piaffe* that Diego had taught her. She didn't get it exactly right, but good enough for a first effort. The important thing was the rhythm worked!

The sound of clapping started her. She looked over to see Helga standing by the fence.

"What was that? Not exactly the Chopin *Polonaise* you were working on with Diego!"

Kelly laughed. "No, but I was thinking—people will be bringing their kids here, and they're liable to get bored with too much classical stuff. Dressage already has an image of being too upper-class and old-fashioned. Maybe we need to bring it into the twenty-first century."

Helga wagged her head, although she kept her smile. "Diego's not going to like that."

"Well, he isn't here, is he? If he can work out his own routine, so can I. Do me a favor, would you? Rewind the tape, so I can try that again!"

*   *   *

Her annoyance with Diego didn't prevent Kelly from doing the best job she could on the flyers to promote the open house. They chose the theme "A Fiesta in Old Spain," and she wrote colorful text inviting visitors to sample authentic Spanish food while watching Andalusian horses perform the highest levels of dressage. Nora, who turned out to have not only culinary but artistic talents, traced an old photo of Bernardo Villaneuva in full Spanish costume, astride a prancing Baslio, for an illustration.

*   *   *

Diego offered to drop off a flyer at the *Sun* on one of his afternoon trips to the Lucky Shot. Getting ready to leave, he promised Kelly, "Starting tomorrow morning, I'm going to work with you on your routine!"

"Don't worry about it," she told him in a cool voice. "I've been practicing on my own. It's coming along just fine."

This remark troubled Diego. They were hoping to draw a hundred people to the open house, maybe more. None of them could afford to turn in a sloppy performance—it would make the horses look bad and defeat the whole purpose. Tactfully, he told Kelly, "I know Gitano is well-trained, but you still need someone on the ground to advise you on the fine points."

She answered with a cocky lift of her chin and eyebrows. "Hmm, yes. Is that what Sandy is doing with you?"

Diego ran out of patience. "Kelly, you're being childish. You're letting your...jealousy, or whatever it is...get in the way of your common sense! You know your freestyle has got to look professional. It won't matter how much you practice, if you practice something wrong."

She just smiled, unmoved. "I'll ask Helga to spot me. She's experienced enough. That way, you won't have to worry about running back here on my account. You can concentrate on your own routine, and Felipe's, and...whatever else you're doing over there."

So angry he couldn't think of a response, Diego vaulted into his SUV, slammed the door and peeled out of the barnyard.

*   *   *

Kelly took pains to make sure all of the ranch's suspected enemies knew about the open house. Sandy, of course, was already well informed. Kelly also mailed a flyer to *Don* Carlos with a graciously worded note personally inviting him to attend.

One crisp midweek morning, she drove to Rio Dorado with her backpack full of flyers. She set out several on a prominently placed rattan table in the lobby, and a few more at the end of the bar in the Twilight Lounge. Feeling bold, she followed the administration corridor to Thorne's private office, hoping to hand him an invitation in person.

She encountered only his assistant, a Ms. Braff from the nameplate on her mahogany desk. "I'm sorry," she said, in a trained, TV-meteorologist voice. "Mr. Thorne is traveling and won't be back until the weekend."

Kelly smiled brightly. "Then he'll be just in time to come to this!" She handed over the flyer and letter. "Please tell him Mr. Villaneuva looks forward to seeing him there."

The assistant nodded slowly, having no idea what she was agreeing to, but Kelly felt sure she would deliver the message.

Having dispersed all the flyers, Kelly felt lighter both physically and mentally as she headed back up the corridor. Her route to the lobby took her past the Twilight Lounge again. Nearing it, she saw someone who'd just come out of the bar pick up one of the flyers. She felt a flutter of elation that already they were attracting attention from the hotel guests. Then the man glanced up and she recognized Thorne's long-haired helicopter pilot.

The same person who just happened to spot Rico's body while flying over Diego's property.

He must've noticed Kelly staring because he met her gaze quizzically, as if unsure whether or not to connect her with the flyer in his hand. Kelly could think of a dozen cutting things to say to him, none of which would serve her purpose of finding out whether Thorne had anything to do with Rico's murder.

Instead, she adopted the same perky tone she'd used on her contacts all morning, telling him as she passed, "It's going to be a fun day. Hope to see you there!"

*   *   *

Back at the barn office, several phone messages awaited. Most came from strangers wanting more information on the open house or directions to the ranch. One especially cryptic one, however, had been left by *Don* Carlos.

His deep, inflected, rolling baritone reminded Kelly of a villain from an old Zorro movie. "Diego, I received your delightful invitation for your very ambitious special event. I must congratulate you on your resourcefulness. You have your father's fighting spirit! If my health permits, I will make every effort to attend. I have a surprise for you, anyway, that I would like to deliver in person. You might call it a parting gift in memory of your father."

Kelly had been scribbling notes for the various messages, but this one froze her pencil in mid-air. She stared at the answering machine while the tape rewound, as if that might help her decipher Salazar's meaning. On the surface, his words sounded innocent, even kindly. Still, that reference to Diego's father—supposedly, Bernardo Villaneuva and *Don* Carlos had hated each other! A gift in Bernardo's memory just might be a destructive one. Kelly also didn't like the terms "surprise" or "parting."

Maybe they'd been too quick to discount the *don* as their saboteur. Kelly only hoped by inviting him to visit the ranch, she hadn't opened them up to yet another blow. One that might shut them down for good.

*   *   *

Around Diego, the arena blurred, as if he were whirling on a carousel. With one hand, he kept *la garocha*, a fourteen-foot wooden pole, anchored in the dirt. With the other, he held Hidalgo's reins. Full of fire and coiled like a spring beneath his rider, the stallion held to a steady, rhythmic canter as he circled the pole like a wheel turning around its axle.

Diego felt dizzy, not only from the spin, but from elation. This was a new move, and in just a few days, Hidalgo had learned it well. Diego could've relished this exhilaration for hours, but he wouldn't abuse his horse's good nature. Almost reluctantly, he brought Hidalgo down to a walk to save his energy for the next day's open house.

At least we'll be ready for our audience, Diego thought. He only wished he felt as sure about Kelly.

She refused to let him even watch her practice, claiming she put in many hours while he was away. She was doing this out of spite, he told himself, to make him crazy! Helga insisted she was helping Kelly, but that didn't completely reassure him. Helga rode well, and could train a horse, but as far as Diego knew she'd never taught riders. He would have felt much more confident if he'd worked with Kelly himself. As things were, he couldn't help fretting, and making vague threats against her in his mind. *I swear, if she does anything to ruin this open house...*

Sandy, watching over the fence, interrupted his broodings with a shout. "Some fancy footwork, *caballero!* Never saw that move before."

He let Hidalgo walk toward her on a loose rein, and dropped the pole near the gate. "*Gracias.* It's Spanish. It comes out of the bullfight—training the horse to circle the bull while the *picador* sticks him with the lances."

"Ouch."

"I know—but it still makes a nice dance step." Diego patted Hidalgo's sweaty, dappled neck. "I think we're as ready as we'll ever be."

Sandy smiled. As usually, she looked fully made-up and coifed, and wore some kind of snug, fringed top. "If you're done practicing, maybe you'd like some supper. Cook's frying up some chicken."

Diego hesitated. He'd accepted the invitation once before, and enjoyed meeting Sandy's staff. Afterward, though, he'd had the impression Kelly and the others didn't appreciate his being away all evening. "Thanks, but I'd better get back. It is the last night before our show. Hidalgo and I may be ready, but I have to make sure everyone else is, too. They've all been complaining I haven't been around much to help them."

Sandy narrowed her aqua-blue eyes in comprehension. "I'm not surprised. I get the feeling none of them are too crazy about me."

Diego held off replying while he vaulted down from Hidalgo's back and unlatched the gate. He supposed Sandy must've sensed some chilliness when Helga or Kelly answered the phone. "That's not really true, Sandy. It's just that they know you'd like to combine our two ranches, and they want Rancho Villaneuva to keep its own identity. As I do."

She nodded, swinging the gate open. "I understand, and maybe I shouldn't have pushed that idea so hard." As he passed, though, she leaned over to squeeze his arm. "But y'know, Diego, even if the ranches stay separate, you and I could still get a little closer."

He sighed. He had figured she'd bring that question out in the open sooner or later. He took stock of Sandy's obvious charms, which he'd always found a little *too* obvious. In the past, he'd compared her unfavorably to the ladylike Isabella. Today, though, he thought instead of Kelly's breezy naturalness...her mischievous giggle...her delicate but very capable figure in boyish riding clothes...the way she seemed innocent of her own sex appeal.

He'd thought often about that last kiss they'd shared in the barn office—the softness of her mouth beneath his, the surprising hunger with which she'd pressed her warm, pliant, little body against him. He'd never wanted that moment to end, and it might not have, if Kelly hadn't turned suddenly shy and pulled away.

Annoyed as Diego was by her latest tactics, he realized in a backhanded way she was doing it because she cared about him. And he thought of how furious she would be if he even considered responding to Sandy's come-on.

Sandy read his face well. "You've gotten over Isabella, but I've got a new rival, don't I? Is there something between you and Kelly?"

He tried to be tactful. "I have feelings for her, yes. After all, she's done so much for me...and for the ranch. She risked her life trying to stop Rico."

"Mmm. I've done a few favors for you, too, and I'd gladly do more. But it's not just gratitude I see in your eyes when you talk about Kelly." Sandy shrugged, then seemed to force a laugh. "Oh, well, to quote my role model Annie Oakley, you can't get a man with a gun. Or, I guess, with a checkbook."

Though he knew he'd made the right decision, Diego still felt like a heel. "Sandy, I am sorry. You've always been a good friend, and I hope that can continue. I just think we need to keep our friendship professional."

"Of course." He noticed, though, she dodged his eyes.

Leading his horse from the ring, he tried to change to subject. "I hope you don't mind keeping these guys one more night. I'll pick them up first thing tomorrow morning."

"No problem." Sandy called out sharply to a groom lounging near her barn. "Steve, put Mr. Villaneuva's horse away for him. He's in a hurry to get back to his place."

This startled Diego because he'd been untacking and grooming the stallions himself. He let the lanky ranch hand take the reins and lead Hidalgo off to the butter-yellow barn.

Sandy finally faced him again, a stiffness in her smile and a hard shine in her eyes. "Don't worry. I'll take good care of your stallions until tomorrow. After all, you've got a lot riding on them—in every sense—don't you?"

When Diego lingered, unsure how to respond, she made a shooing motion with her brightly manicured fingers.

Not wanting to act suspicious of her, he got in his Range Rover and headed home. Allusions to temperamental mares filled his mind. Stallions had the bad reputation, but a mare in season could be just as dangerous! He felt caught between two headstrong females, either of who could ruin everything he'd worked for.

The question was, did he have more to fear from Sandy, or from Kelly?

CHAPTER 21

Kelly surveyed her appearance in her full-length bedroom mirror and succumbed to a wave of panic. She shouldn't be doing this…it was all wrong! She should change into her usual dressage show clothes— black helmet, white stock shirt, black jacket and white breeches—and do the classical freestyle routine Diego had mapped out for her.

Instead she stood, ready to perform in public to a soft-rock tape, wearing stretch black breeches with a bright turquoise pattern up the sides, a matching stretch cover on her helmet and a bright turquoise T-shirt. Even though it was all riding gear from Aiken's Feed Store, she looked like a cartoon superhero. *All I need is a big H on my chest for Horsewoman!*

Everyone else, she knew, would be dressed in either neutral riding clothes or Spanish attire, in keeping with the Fiesta in Old Spain theme. Well, she would have looked even more ridiculous, with her red hair and freckles, decked out in the kind of Spanish ruffles Isabella had worn so well. If her outfit and routine might shock Diego, they also might come as a pleasant surprise for the visitors.

Anyway, there was no changing now, when she'd practiced her new freestyle for weeks and Diego's not at all. With a last, anxious glance in the mirror, Kelly mustered her courage to go outside and literally face the music.

She stepped out of her bungalow to see the barnyard area teeming with people. For a few minutes, all misgivings left her mind as she realized her efforts had paid off. She'd worked hard to attract people to this event, and they'd turned out in even higher numbers than she'd expected! She saw strangers of all ages, from suntanned senior citizens to young couples pushing babies in strollers.

Then she thought of the flip side. If she made a fool of herself with her freestyle, she'd be doing it in front of a lot of people.

She felt grateful Sheriff Michaels had lent them several uniformed officers for the day. The cops looked relaxed and unobtrusive, but they held down key spots by the barn and the main ring. *They might come in handy,* thought Kelly. *In case* Don *Carlos or anyone else pulls any last-minute "surprises."*

She passed the refreshment table where Nora and her cousin Alicia were making and selling Spanish culinary specialties, including *empanadas*—turnovers with spicy beef filling—and *banderillas,* which looked like shish kebabs.

Suddenly Kelly spied a head with long, brown hair and a rather Streisand-ish profile that looked familiar, and called out, "Judy, is that you?"

Her former co-worker spun around, almost choking on a bite of her fresh *empanada.* She wore denim shorts and a striped T-shirt, and Kelly realized it was the first time she'd seen Judy in anything but work clothes. She kept the food out of the way while she hugged Kelly and said, "I was looking all over for you!"

"I just went back to my bungalow to change."

Judy stepped back to get the full effect of the outfit, and gave a low whistle. "Lookin' good! I thought dressage riders always wore stuffy black-and-white outfits. You look like you're ready for a bike race!"

Kelly made a wry face. "I know. It's kind of a surprise, and I'm afraid Diego's going to kill me."

"Speaking of Diego, I may have seen him. Is he the hunky creature who was showing people through the barn about half an hour ago?"

Kelly laughed. "Must've been. No offense to Alonzo or Felipe, but Diego's the only resident on the premises who fits that description."

Judy shot her a teasing, under-the-lashes look. "I don't think you've told me half of what's been going on around here!"

Kelly clapped her on the shoulder. "You'd better believe it. If I only told you half, it would take hours! And unfortunately, I have to go get ready for my freestyle…uh, performance. I'll catch you up later."

"Promise?"

"I swear. And thanks so much for coming!"

Kelly passed the outdoor ring where the demonstrations had already begun. Helga was lunging Turi in side reins while explaining the benefits to her audience.

In the barn, Kelly found Diego bridling Belleza for his long-reining demo. He wore his usual riding garb of deep-toned polo shirt—maroon, today—gray breeches and boots. As Kelly passed, he raised his eyebrows, but made no comment.

She led Gitano from his stall and put him on crossties farther down the aisle. She'd threaded his lush, copper mane and tail with turquoise ribbons to match her own outfit. The mode of decoration was Spanish enough, but not the color.

Without even looking over, she felt Diego staring at her. Finally he said, "Aren't you going to look a little strange in that getup, riding to Chopin and Mozart?"

"We're not riding to Chopin and Mozart. We're riding to Steve Winwood."

"Who?"

Helga returned, leading Turi, just in time to overhear their dialogue. "Don't worry, Diego. She'll be fine."

This didn't mollify him. "Kelly, I thought at least you were practicing the freestyle we worked on together. I didn't think you were going to make up something by yourself!"

Although she was actually trembling by now with anxiety, Kelly faked a careless shrug. "I figure it'll be a good balance. Your ride will be very traditional, and mine will be modern. People will see dressage can be versatile."

Even in the barn shadows, she saw his face redden. "You're just doing this to get even with me, for—"

Helga tapped him on the arm and bobbed her head towards the open barn door. "Diego, better hurry. The crowd's waiting."

He said nothing more, but furiously finished tacking up Belleza and took her away. Kelly hoped the high-strung mare wouldn't pick up on his bad mood and misbehave in front of the audience.

Kelly glanced at Helga for reassurance. "Maybe this whole thing was a bad idea."

"Too late to change your mind now."

"I know. You'll be cuing up the music, right?"

Helga nodded. "For you and Diego. It's my big chance to play DJ. By the way, I think I spotted *Don* Carlos out there."

That refocused Kelly's attention. "No kidding?" Earlier, she had seen Sandy wandering around. So two out of three suspects had arrived as expected!

"Funny," added Helga, "he was carrying some kind of briefcase."

"Oh, no," said Kelly, only half-joking.

"Why?"

"He promised Diego a big surprise today. I sure hope it isn't a bomb!"

Alonzo trudged in with Belleza in tow. The mare was breathing hard and rolling her eyes, and Alonzo shook his head.

"How did she do?" Kelly asked him.

"She start out good. Everybody 'ooh' and 'aah' over how pretty she is. Then some kid stick a teddy bear on top of the fence." Alonzo shot an exasperated look at the mare. "She jump sideways and almos' trample Diego."

"Oh, God! Is he okay?"

"*Si*. Diego fast on his feet. He make the good save, and they finished all right. He up t' the house now, changing his clothes."

Helga looked at Kelly. "Almost time, girl. It's Felipe, then you."

"I know."

Kelly finished tacking up Gitano and brought him outside. A few people pointed and smiled at the gelding's showy coloring and bright ribbons. While she warmed him up in one of the paddocks, Kelly noticed Felipe skillfully guiding Basilio over a course of low hurdles in the main ring. For someone who'd only been taking jumping lessons for three months, Felipe had made terrific progress, and piloted the stallion like an expert.

Near the gate, Kelly ran into Sandy, decked out even more authentically then usual. In addition to her white Stetson, cowboy boot earrings, fringed shirt and tight jeans, she wore an actual leather holster around her waist. Complete with an actual revolver.

"Well!" She appraised Kelly's getup. "If this is part of Old Spain, I must've missed my history class that day."

"Just a little something to get the kids' attention." Kelly, in return, eyeballed Sandy's gun. "Is that the real thing?"

Sandy whipped it out and twirled it like a practiced gunslinger. "Colt.45. A replica, but a working one. It's loaded, too."

Kelly backed a step. "Is it legal?"

"Sure. I have a permit and it's not concealed. I figured you guys need all the security you can get today." She holstered the revolver again with a meaningful glance at Kelly. "Don't worry. I wouldn't dream of disrupting your fiesta with any unnecessary gunplay. I'm a better sport than that. I don't lose often, but I hope I know how to do it gracefully."

"Lose? What do you mean?"

Sandy smiled with a sharp edge. "Diego and you. I'll admit, I put up a good fight, but I know when I'm beat. Of course, you had the home field advantage, didn't you? If I were living on the ranch with him, seeing him day and night, I could find ways to make him fall for me, too!"

Kelly's mouth dropped open. She quickly shut it again to conceal her shock. *Did Diego turn Sandy down, and tell her it was because of me? Sure sounds that way. If only Sandy knew how little chance I had to press my home field advantage!*

"You're probably right," Kelly admitted. "At any rate, I'm glad to hear there are no hard feelings." With another glance at the .45, she added, "Especially while you're toting that!"

Sandy laughed. "I'm saving that for your saboteur. I think I've figured out who he is, and if he makes a move today, I'll be ready."

Abruptly, Kelly's cool façade crumbled and she started to babble. "You did? You have? Who—?"

"Oh, no, I'm not telling. Have to hang on to some advantage of my own!" When Kelly looked eager to press the question, Sandy cut her off. "Besides, don't you have to perform now?"

She was right, Kelly admitted. There was no time. Felipe had left the ring, and the crowd watched the empty space in expectation.

She led Gitano over to the mounting block, swung onto his back and rode towards the gate. Meanwhile, though, her mind whirled. *Sandy thinks she knows the identity of our saboteur? And Diego told her—what? That he cares for me? Loves me?*

Do I feel the same way about him?

Kelly warned herself she couldn't deal with any of those questions at the moment. She had to push them away and concentrate totally on her ride.

She saw Helga watching from the window of the barn office and waved to signal her. She totted Gitano down the center line of the ring and stopped in the middle, waiting for the tape to start. She reflected it was a good thing she knew this routine so well, or Sandy's comments might have driven the whole thing out of her head!

The first downbeat sent a quiver of anxiety through Kelly's stomach, but after that, she settled down to business. She trotted the rest of the way down the center and made a sharp left at the fence. Up the long side they went in a shoulder-in, with Gitano cruising sideways as easily as if he were rolling on ball bearings. A turn at the corner, then haunches-in down the other long side. They hit the next corner just in time to mark the crescendo with an extended trot across the diagonal. Gitano chugged through that one like a machine, throwing out his front legs and really covering ground.

Down the quarter line, half-pass left to the other quarter line, then back again, in a nice zigzag. His shoulder bowed out a little too much towards the end, but no time to correct—it was all going by too fast.

The tape segued into the canter music, and Gitano took off crisply at the corner. They did a three-loop serpentine, and the lead changes went okay. An extended canter across the diagonal set the streamers in his mane flying. More half-passes at the center—those went well—and another turn at the corner.

Okay, pal, here goes nothing!

Down the diagonal again, at the canter, and then their toughest challenge—flying changes every three strides. Kelly knew she had to be sharp here. Left leg back, one, two; right leg back, one, two...*Damn, missed that one, I'll add it at the end.*

Skip...Skip...Skip...

They hit the fence line and, even before Kelly could ask, Gitano made the extra change on his own so he would be balanced for the turn. At the top of the ring, they cantered a half-pirouette, which brought them around again to face the gate. The music changed back to four-four, and they downshifted into another strong trot. Kelly collected him in the middle of the ring for *passage. Good boy, Gitano!* They wound up with the *piaffe,* Kelly pushing him into a nice, high step. Right on the song's last beat, it became a good, square halt.

Ecstatic over having pulled it off with only a few glitches, Kelly went for the *pièce de resistance.* She used her long dressage whip to tap Gitano on the shoulder. He sank into a deep bow, his be-ribboned mane tumbling forward over his eyes.

The crowd not only clapped but whooped and cheered, which made the horse snap upright again in some alarm. A flurry of grateful pats from Kelly steadied him, though. He walked out of the ring with dignity like the star he was.

Kelly basked in a moment of glory as Felipe and Alonzo congratulated her. Judy also showed up to gush, "That was amazing, Kel! I didn't know you could ride like that."

Dismounting, she patted Gitano again. "Hey, give some credit to my buddy here. He's a dancing fool! And, of course, I've learned a lot working with Diego." Her eyes scanned the barnyard. "By the way, is he around?"

"Last I saw, he was over there talking to some man with a briefcase."

Kelly followed Judy's pointing finger. It took her a minute to even recognize Diego. He'd changed into full Spanish costume, including black suede boots, *toreador*-style, high-waisted pants, white ruffled shirt and embroidered *bolero*.

If he looked handsome under ordinary circumstances, Kelly thought, dressed like this he'd make any woman with a heartbeat swoon!

In one hand, he held the same kind of round-brimmed hat his father wore in those old photos. He stood in conversation with a heavy-set, jowly man who also wore a ruffled shirt, but with a more conventional black suit, and carried a slim, brown briefcase.

That has to be Don *Carlos,* Kelly thought. Studying the two, she didn't detect any signs of hostility. After a minute, the older man passed Diego the briefcase, they shook hands and Diego actually smiled.

They parted company then, and Diego called Felipe to bring Hidalgo over. The stallion wore the Bernardo Villaneuva's exotic Spanish saddle, with red ribbons braided into his mane and tail. Diego handed Felipe the briefcase and Kelly heard him tell the boy to put it in the barn office.

She jogged up to Diego and asked, "Are you sure that's a good idea? Have you checked to see if it's ticking?"

He laughed. "I've already seen what's inside. It's a surprise, all right, but no bomb. It's the papers for three of his top broodmares."

"What?"

"He's retiring, and he's selling them to me at rock-bottom prices, a big loss for him. He also threw in a list of names and phone numbers of all his former customers."

Kelly stared. "Wow, that's some change of heart. What do you think happened?"

Diego squinted thoughtfully in the hot afternoon sunshine. "He says now that he's sick himself, he feels sorry he let my father die with bad blood still between them. I guess this is his way of trying to make things right."

"Fantastic!" The three mares, Kelly thought, would almost make up for the ones Diego had lost. And all of those extra customers—if they panned out—would also be a big help.

Before she dared to ask, Diego answered her unspoken question. "By the way, about your freestyle…"

Kelly's heart pounded in her throat. *I knew it. Just when I wanted to make things right between us, I've gone and pissed him off.*

"You know," he continued sternly, "if you had asked me first, I would have told you not to ride to that kind of music."

She swallowed hard, like a child bracing herself to be scolded by an adored parent. She didn't like the unequal feeling…but she suppose she wanted Diego's approval, after all. "I know."

"So…I guess it's a good thing you didn't ask me."

When she searched his face, he grinned broadly.

"You mean it was okay?"

"Terrific, considering you did it all yourself. And you may have been right about our audience. From what I overheard, everybody loved it. I'm almost sorry I have to follow you!"

"Oh, I think you and Hidalgo are up to it."

"We'll do our best." He popped the flat-brimmed, *toreador*-style hat on his head, tilting it to shade his eyes mysteriously. "You and *Don* Carlos aren't the only ones around here capable of pulling a few surprises!"

CHAPTER 22

When Diego rode into the ring on Hidalgo, both of them in full Spanish regalia, people flocked back to the fence as if magnetized. Kelly had to worm herself into a gap where she could actually see something. For once she felt thankful she was small—and pushy.

Helga started Diego's music, a throbbing *flamenco* guitar in a minor key, with an almost Middle Eastern feeling. Hidalgo stepped into his working trot, giving it a bit more *macho* swagger than Gitano had done. Having ridden that kind of strong trot herself, Kelly marveled at the easy way Diego sat to it, tall and straight as a statue. Somehow, his exotic costume underscored the excellence of his riding, turning him into the very image of Old World perfection.

Close behind her, Kelly heard someone say, "Ms. Sheridan!"

She turned to face Gavin Thorne and surprise knocked the wind out of her. Not having spotted him up to then, she'd decided he wasn't going to show.

He wore an open-necked, lemon-yellow shirt under a beige gabardine jacket, and a genial smile. "I understand I have you to thank for inviting me here today. That was very thoughtful."

Kelly noticed two men hovering in back of him. One she didn't recognize—he hid his eyes behind aviator sunglasses, and his dark suit spanned the glacial physique of a bodyguard. The other was Joe Eagle, who'd matched his long ponytail with a black shirt and jeans.

Kelly wondered what the pilot was doing there. Thorne couldn't have come to the ranch by chopper—they all would have noticed the commotion. Kelly figured he'd arrived in the white limo parked out by the entrance, and the menacing guy in the sunglasses must be his driver. Was Thorne so worried about Joe's drinking he couldn't let him out of his sight?

Then Kelly noticed something else about the pilot's turnout. He wore a black Stetson hat with a speckled feather in the band. In every respect but the color, it was identical to the one she'd found in the *arroyo*.

Once she noticed that, it took Kelly an extra minute to regain her poise and answer Thorne. "You're welcome. We were hoping you could make it. After all, we are neighbors."

Thorne shook his head in amusement. "I also understand you left brochures all over my lobby. I imagine a lot of your guests here today came from Rio Dorado. There was such a migration towards your ranch, all I had to do was follow the herd."

"I hope I didn't overstep my bounds. After all, your guests are just the kind of people we'd like to reach—sports-minded and affluent. The kind who might be interested in buying our horses."

Out of the corner of her eye, Kelly watched Diego execute a couple of full canter pirouettes on Hidalgo. His precision impressed her as always. From the spontaneous applause, it impressed the crowd, too.

"I admit," Thorne went on, "I was surprised to hear you were holding such a public event. Wasn't this ranch quarantined just a couple of months ago?"

He said this rather loudly, as if to make himself heard over the music, and Kelly saw a few nearby heads turn. One of them was Sandy Garrett's. Kelly maintained her cordial tone. "Fortunately, that turned out to be a complete false alarm. The vet gave all of our horses clean bills of health."

Sandy intruded then, her pitch also a bit louder than necessary. "That's right. I've actually been keeping two of Diego's horses at my ranch for the past couple of weeks. I wouldn't have done that if I thought they were contagious!"

Thorne raised his eyebrows, a look of concession. "No, I guess not."

Another burst of applause turned Kelly's eyes back to the ring. Diego wound up his canter work with flying lead changes across the diagonal. Kelly had found it difficult enough to do a change every three strides, but Diego had Hidalgo doing changes every other stride. The stallion skipped across the ring with springing power, in perfect rhythm

160

with the fiery, pulsing music.

Didn't miss a one! Kelly thought, envying Diego's skill.

Thorne interrupted again. "By the way, what was the deal with that body Joe spotted on your property? Ever get to the bottom of that?"

Kelly ground her molars. Not only was he interfering with her enjoyment of Diego's performance, he was deliberately bringing up every controversial subject that might embarrass her, and in a voice loud enough for the other guests to overhear. If he thought she'd be too shaken to spar back, though, he had another think coming. Without even looking over her shoulder, she said, "Yes—that's still a mystery. We have no idea who he was, or how he got out there."

She heard a pause, and hoped she'd thrown Thorne a curve. "Doesn't it worry you, though?"

"Of course. That's one reason why Ms. Garrett took a couple of our horses temporarily, so we'd have fewer to look out for." Kelly nodded in Sandy's direction. "And we asked the police to post some guards here at the ranch. As you can see, there are still a few here today."

Now the *flamenco* music slowed and Diego put Hidalgo into the Spanish walk. The stallion kicked out dramatically with each foreleg, in perfect time to the staccato chords of the guitar.

Thorne persisted. "They couldn't identify the dead man at all? Didn't he have any I.D. on him?"

Spiders crawled up Kelly's spine. She felt sure now she was talking to their real saboteur, and that Thorne had masterminded all of their problems. She felt no qualms about lying to a liar. "Guess not. And his face was so messed up he was unrecognizable."

That information shut Thorne up for a while. The next voice Kelly heard was Joe Eagle asking, "They got anything around here to drink?"

Kelly piped up cheerfully. "Juice and soft drinks at that booth with the striped awning."

Thorne laughed. "Just as well for you, Joe! Bring me a bottled water while you're at it." Kelly noticed he didn't give the pilot any money.

In the ring, Hidalgo sat back in a *levade* with Diego still aboard. Their pose reminded Kelly of the moment she'd seen Diego for the first time. Less than six months, but how much had happened since then! And she still had no idea how it would all end.

Her gadfly, Thorne, chuckled again. "You're lucky the police didn't accuse any of you of murdering that fellow! After all, he was found on your land."

"Mmm... Fortunately, we were able to convince them none of us had any reason to do such a thing."

Hidalgo stretched taller on his hind legs and Kelly realized Diego intended to ride him through the *courbette*. Seeing him perched so high on the temperamental stallion, she suddenly feared for his safety. She reminded herself they probably had practiced this a million times.

Hidalgo hopped on his powerful hind legs once...twice...three times...then dropped to all fours again. Everyone cheered and Kelly exhaled. Why had she been so worried about Diego?

Because she loved him, she realized. She really did.

When Hidalgo sat back again, she knew Diego had to be setting him up for the grand finale, the *capriole*. Kelly couldn't believe he was actually going to stay aboard for that. She almost wanted to shut her eyes...except she couldn't bear to miss the spectacle. To a crescendo from the recorded guitar, the stallion leaped high into the air and kicked straight backward. He hovered for an instant like a huge, silver bird, mane and tail fanning out like flames, Diego straight and still on his back. Hidalgo landed again to wild applause, which sent him spinning in an unplanned half-pirouette. Diego quieted his mount with a pat, and his stony expression finally broke into a grin.

"Whoa!" said Thorne, more to his driver than to Kelly. "I wouldn't want to get in the way of that kick, would you?"

Another shot at Diego, Kelly fumed. *Another lame attempt to make him look capable of murdering Rico.* She only hoped the cops posted near the ring weren't thinking along the same lines. The last thing Diego needed now was for the sheriff to start suspecting him again!

Kelly decided she'd put up with enough of Thorne's ill-disguised heckling. She wanted to congratulate Diego on his wonderful ride, and maybe even whisper her real feelings in his ear. "Excuse me," she told Thorne and his driver.

On her way towards the gate, she spotted Joe still waiting in line at the refreshment stand. She had an inspiration and, although she knew it might amount to nothing, she dodged back to her own bungalow.

A few minutes later, she intercepted the pilot as he was leaving with his can of Coke and a bottle of Poland Spring. "I saw you over at Rio Dorado the day I was putting out my brochures. Got your attention, eh?"

Joe hesitated, as if trying to think of the smooth thing to say. "The boss invited us along today. Thought it would be the neighborly thing to do."

"That's a great hat!" She pointed with one hand, keeping the other behind her back. "Funniest thing—a couple of months ago, I found one exactly like that on our back property." She produced the battered Stetson. "See? Identical, except for the color! Even the same kind of feather in the band. Bet it would have the same label...maybe it's even the same size. Of course, this one's in awful shape. It was half buried in the dirt. Could've been there a year or more!"

It pleased her to see the color drain from Joe's strong-boned, bronze cheeks. "That's a coincidence all right."

"Isn't it? This hat was at the bottom of the *arroyo*. Doesn't belong to anyone on our ranch. I keep wondering who could've lost it there...and what he was doing on our property."

"That's a real mystery." Joe tried to veer around her with his drinks. In spite of her shorter statue, Kelly blocked his way like a cow pony cutting off a steer.

"I lied to your boss, you know. About the man found dead on our property. We know who he was, and we know he wasn't working alone. So if you had anything to do with his murder, you'd be smart to come clean now."

It was the biggest bluff she'd pulled since the day she got herself hired at Rancho Villaneuva. To her amazement, this brazen trick worked just as well. The pilot's shoulders sagged in resignation. He handed her the bottle of water meant for his boss, and dropped his voice. "Okay, I'll tell you everything, on one condition—I want one of the cops here as a witness."

"You do?" Dazed by this second surprise, Kelly waved over the nearest of Michaels' deputies.

Eagle told the young, sandy-haired guard, "I want to make a confession. I dropped that body on Diego Villaneuva's property from my helicopter."

Shocked at first, Kelly saw the logic of it. No tire tracks anywhere, just hoofprints left over from their previous rides. It also explained how Diego could have been riding in the area at the time Farley had died, yet seen no sign of the corpse. It was deposited later.

Joe told her, "Thorne had Farley killed and made me dump the body to frame Diego. Thorne's behind all the stuff that's been going wrong at your ranch."

Finally hearing this stated as a fact, Kelly almost trembled with relief. "I thought so, but we never had any proof."

The pilot laughed harshly. "I can get you proof—as long as you'll

163

give me protection."

"Protection?" the guard asked.

"From Thorne! If he could ice Farley, he could do the same to me."
Eagle swung around, eyes searching the crowd. "Look—he must've
seen me talking to you!"

Kelly saw Thorne and his driver striding away from the main ring
as quickly as they could without being too obvious. She knew they
must be headed for the limo.

A loud snort made her jump, and she looked up into the big, liquid
eye of Hidalgo. Diego leaned down from his saddle to ask, "What's
going on?"

Kelly pointed. "It's Thorne, Diego! It's been him all along...and
he's getting away!"

That was all Diego needed to hear. He put his heels into his horse's
sides and gave chase.

They looped around the startled spectators and galloped for the
entrance archway. Kelly jogged after them, and she could see Sandy
had also started to chase Thorne. No one, though, was a match for
Hidalgo. At the last minute, he cut between the two men on foot and
the white limo. Thorne and his driver tried to dodge away, but Diego
trapped them like a *picador* circling a bull, keeping his horse at an even
canter so they couldn't escape.

Kelly saw the driver reach inside his coat, and gasped. "Diego,
watch out!"

Just then, Sandy reached the entrance and pulled her own revolver.
"Don't even think about it, pal."

When the driver dropped his gun, and both he and Thorne put their
hands in the air, Diego backed Hidalgo to a safe distance. He couldn't
resist, however, putting in him into one last *levade* and doffing his
black *toreador* hat at the gawking crowd.

Kelly did her best to salvage the situation, and gave the stunned
onlookers her best p.r. smile. "As you can see, folks, dressage also has
its practical uses. You can round up cattle...and all kinds of pesky
varmints!"

*   *   *

An hour later, at the police station, Joe Eagle told his full story to
Sheriff Michaels, Kelly and Diego. From time to time, he rubbed the
back of his sunburned neck, as if he felt a guillotine blade bearing
down on him.

"Thorne felt Rico bungled that last job at your ranch. He was seen and recognized. Sooner or later, he was bound to get caught, and then he'd rat on Thorne in a minute to save his own skin. On top of that, Farley never even did what he was supposed to do."

Diego's spirits lifted, even though this confirmed what he already knew. "He never injected the horse?"

"No, and he was actually stupid enough to admit that to Thorne. So Thorne had him whacked and made me dispose of the body." The pilot massaged his face with both hands now in a weary gesture. "When I saw that, I knew there was nothing to stop him from doing the same to me. That's why I figure I got nothing to lose by turnin' myself in. He's laid too much on my conscience, man. More than I can live with."

Diego couldn't help a cynical response. "Don't flog yourself over Rico. He was pretty worthless. Anyway, you didn't kill him."

"No, not him. If it was only Rico, I wouldn't feel so bad. But then there was the business last year, with your wife…"

A jolt of electricity shot through Diego, as if he were standing in water and someone had just dropped in a live wire. His voice came out as a strangled whisper. "What?"

"It was an accident. I wanted to help her, but Thorne wouldn't let me. And I listened to him."

Diego couldn't speak, and Michaels chose not to. It was left to Kelly to coax the pilot on. "What…exactly…happened?"

On the day of Isabella's death, Joe told them, he was flying Thorne and an architect over the back twenty acres of Rancho Villaneuva. Thorne wanted to build a cluster of time-share villas, and had just learned he couldn't use his own undeveloped acreage because it harbored a rare species of lizard. This made him turn his sights toward Diego's property. He wanted the architect to scope it out for him and assess its potential before he made a serious bid.

The chopper was hovering low near the *arroyo,* so the architect could judge its depth, when Isabella rode onto the scene.

"She was goin' full gallop like she was blowin' off steam or somethin'," Joe recalled. "Then I guess her horse saw the chopper or heard the noise, and spooked big time. Spun around so hard the whole saddle came off. Your wife fell off, too, and rolled all the way down into that gully."

Diego listened with a tight throat, reliving secondhand the fatal scene he'd never witnessed.

"From the air, we all saw her fall. I wanted to land and see if she was all right. I started to, but Thorne kept yelling at me to forget it and go back to the resort." Joe's big eyes filled at the memory. "I said we should take her to a doctor, or at least back to your ranch. He said, 'You do that an' Villaneuva will know we were checkin' out his land!'

"I said we could make up some story, but Thorne wouldn't listen. He made like he was goin' to grab the controls himself. So...I flew back to Rio Dorado. Later, I heard she died."

Diego thought of all the blame he'd heaped on Rico and himself. They both still deserved some, but Gavin Thorne deserved a lot more.

Kelly must have sensed his distress. She reached across the table to clasp his hand.

Sheriff Michaels asked Joe, "How did Farley hook up with Thorne?"

"He came lookin' for a maintenance job after he got blackballed from all the ranches. When Thorne found out who he was, he met with Farley personally. I guess that's when he got the idea he could pressure Diego to sell by putting a crimp in his business. And who better to do it than an ex-employee who hated Diego's guts?"

"How do you know Thorne ordered the sabotage? Did you overhear any of their conversations?"

Joe shook his head. "Thorne was too smart for that, but Farley talked to me about it. I guess he thought we were both in the same boat, doin' Thorne's dirty work for him. But I never wanted to. Made me sick when I heard that poor woman died. Probably what started me drinkin'."

Diego heard all of this as if from under water. He was still submerged in his own agony.

Isabella didn't have to die. The men in the helicopter could have saved her...but they'd chosen not to.

Still focused on Joe, Michaels scribbled something on the yellow legal pad in front of him. "So with Farley dead, we have only your word for all this. Yours against Thorne's."

"You might be able to get that architect to testify about Mrs. Villaneuva's accident. If he's anything like me, he's had that day on his conscience, too. I can tell you where to reach him. An' then there's the lab at the college."

"College?"

"Mr. Thorne's *alma mater*. That's where he got the virus to use on the horses."

Diego sent Michaels a hard stare.

The sheriff answered with a look of apology. He told Joe, "We'll get right on that."

"Remember, I want protection. Until Thorne's behind bars. That driver of his, too."

Michaels agreed to this, then faced Diego. "Mr. Villaneuva, I guess that bears up everything you told us. I'm sorry if you got even more painful news today than you expected."

Diego acknowledged this with a short nod. "Have you got Thorne here at the station? I'd like to speak to him."

The sheriff wasn't fooled by Diego's polite tone. Gently but firmly, he said, "I don't think that would be a good idea."

"He's got money and influence. How do I know he won't get away with this?"

"He's also got a stack of charges against him, including conspiracy and murder. I promise you, he's not going anywhere." Michaels called in one of his young deputies. "Mr. Villaneuva is leaving, Tom. Will you see him out?"

On his way out of the room with Kelly at his side, he heard Joe Eagle call after him, "Diego...I really am sorry."

He did not turn around.

*   *   *

"Whatever they do to Thorne, it won't be bad enough," Diego fumed on the drive home.

Quietly, Kelly agreed. "Not unless they break his neck and leave him to die at the bottom of a ravine."

"When I caught up with him this afternoon, I should have let Hidalgo trample him. The cold-hearted son of a bitch!"

Kelly leaned over to rub his shoulder, and he felt suddenly sorry for venting on her...but also grateful he could. He didn't know what he would have done, at this moment, without her. Maybe it was fate that had allowed him to fall in love again before he found out the truth about Isabella, to at least cushion the blow a little.

A bit less ferociously, he went on. "If they only had stopped that day and gotten her to a doctor, or even brought her to the ranch...she might have lived. Can you imagine that man being so callous? To just fly away and leave her?"

"Do you mean Thorne or Joe Eagle?"

"Eagle, too. He knew it was wrong, but he let himself be pressured into it."

"Well, don't be too hard on Joe. If it weren't for his confession, you might never have nailed Thorne."

"He could be making up that story about wanting to help Isabella, just to make himself look good."

"Maybe," Kelly said slowly. "But I think he's telling the truth. I have a feeling he put up a good fight. I think he had the copter door open and was ready to land. But he got into a tussle with Thorne, and was worried he might crash. That's the only reason he took off again."

Diego stared at her, wondering when she'd developed second sight. "How could you know a thing like that?"

"I don't for sure. But it would explain how he lost his hat."

EPILOGUE

One Year Later

"Here he comes!" crowed Helga, kneeling in the straw near the mare. "There's the head!"

Kelly leaned closer to watch the birth, peering over Diego's shoulder. He and Helga were doing the most to help the mare because they had experience. Kelly had never watched a horse give birth before, and held her breath for fear of jinxing things.

The front legs emerged first, lined up neatly under the foal's slick head. Inside the birth sac, Kelly noticed pale, gelatinous pads covering the hooves and pointed them out in alarm.

Diego laughed. "That's normal. They'll fall off later."

Kelly breathed easier. She couldn't help worrying. This was the first birth at Rancho Villaneuva since the four mares had been poisoned and since Kelly had arrived. Had a year-and-a-half passed already? Sometimes it seemed like just a short while. At other times, she felt as if she'd lived here forever.

This was also the first birth to one of the mares Diego had bought from *Don* Carlos. His foals had a tendency towards knock knees, a condition that would be tricky and expensive to correct. Don Carlos had assured Diego the trait came from one of his stallions, and none of his mares carried the gene. Since this foal had been sired by Hidalgo, they would soon know whether *Don* Carlos had told the truth—when the foal tried to stand.

169

The rest of the baby came out, and Diego announced, "It's a colt!"

Good, Kelly thought. If he could be left ungelded, he might become a future sire.

She shifted for a better view and grinned. The wet, lop-eared, awkward, little creature looked gorgeous to her. His coat was dark brown now, but with two gray parents he would probably lighten to gray also. That bony frame would muscle up, and that damp, wispy mane and tail would fill out to full Andalusian splendor.

Diego's voice cut through her reverie. "Kelly, get the wash bucket, so we can clean her up." He meant the mare, who'd just expelled the afterbirth.

Kelly bounced up to fetch the bucket of water, already laced with disinfectant, glad to finally be of help. This healthy birth should be just the first of several. They needed this new crop of foals to insure the future of the ranch.

Over the past year, they'd gradually worked their way back into the black. Showing the horses around the state, they'd won some good ribbons and attracted more business. Kelly had gotten so many blues on Gitano that Diego had given her the freckled gelding as a wedding present. It had been one of many pleasant surprises that day. The biggest, though, was her mother actually flying out from New Jersey for the ceremony.

While Kelly washed the mare, Diego held the foal in plain sight so its dam wouldn't become anxious. As soon as he let go, the colt struggled to stand. Diego and Helga gave him room because it was generally best to let a new foal get up on its own, learning by trial and error.

Kelly knew this, but still fought the temptation to help. "C'mon, little guy, you can do it!"

After collapsing back into the straw a couple of times, the colt finally stayed upright. He swayed on his long legs for a minute, then tottered over to his mother to nurse.

Diego stole closer, and squinted in the glow of the work lamp that hung nearby. "Hard to tell this early, but his legs look fine to me."

Helga smiled. "That's 'cause he's got the right Daddy!" She went to toss out the dirty water, leaving Diego and Kelly alone in the stall.

"You still don't quite believe it, do you?" Kelly teased him. "The 'curse' is over, Diego! Your luck is changing."

He wrapped a strong arm around her waist. "I should trust it by now, shouldn't I? My luck started to change day you came here."

She snuggled against his side. "I can't take all the credit. At least some should go to that nice judge who put Gavin Thorne behind bars."

Far from plaguing them the way Thorne had, the new owner of Rio Dorado wanted to work out a deal so the resort's patrons could ride at Diego's ranch. He planned to board half a dozen horses at Rancho Villaneuva and lease ten of the unused acres for Western trail rides. The proceeds would see them through nicely until the new foals got old enough to train and sell.

Even better, the resort's new owner, a dashing Texan, had hit it off big time with Sandy Garrett.

"I also have to thank *Don* Carlos for selling me his mares," said Diego. "Two of the others are also in foal to Hidalgo. In a few more months, we'll be up to our ears in new babies."

Kelly smiled slyly up at him, and took his hand. "You don't know the half of it!"

Diego gave her a puzzled look.

"Guess now's as good a time to tell you as ever. According to all the home tests I've taken this week—I'm pregnant."

EILEEN WATKINS

Growing up in Cranford, NJ, Eileen Watkins always aspired to write novels. Her earliest efforts involved adventure stories about horses, or Nancy Drew-type mysteries.

In her freshman year at Marywood College in Scranton, PA, she won first place in a college-wide short story contest. She went on after graduation to publish short stories in the magazines *Belladonna* and *Doppleganger*. Excerpts from her unpublished novels won her first prize in a national contest sponsored in 1994 by the Garden State Horror Writers, and second prize in a contest at the 2000 Philadelphia Writer's Conference. In 2003 she published the horror novel *Dance With The Dragon* through Amber Quill Press, as E. F. Watkins.

Eileen is a founding member of, and publicity officer for, the Garden State Horror Writers. She is also a member of the Horror Writers Association, Sisters in Crime/Central Jersey and The Writer's Workshop, Englewood, NJ.

A professional journalist for more than 20 years, Eileen covered art, architecture and interior design for *The Star-Ledger* of Newark, NJ. She now freelances, writing on these same subjects. She shares her 1922 house in northern New Jersey with two cats—Bela and Harley. A lifelong horseback rider, she studies and has competed in dressage.

*   *   *

Don't miss* Black Flowers, *by Eileen Watkins (writing as E.F. Watkins), available Winter 2004 from Amber Quill Press, LLC

When a former employee of her husband's genetic engineering firm dies of a drug overdose on her front lawn, Allison Constantine is horrified. She can't forget the young man's final threats that "people like her" will soon "get what's coming to them."

In the days to come, Allie suspects she's being followed, and fears someone might be trying to kidnap her or her two small children. But who? A rival firm, hoping to extort technical secrets from her husband, David? A protest group that has accused Genesis of reckless experiments? Or a former Genesis president who supposedly killed himself two years earlier?

Probing the company's activities, Allie discovers a pattern of mysterious deaths by electrocution. She fears the greatest threat to her family may be David himself, if she dares to interfere with his terrifying secret plans for his company, society...and even his own children.

AMBER QUILL PRESS, LLC
THE GOLD STANDARD IN PUBLISHING

QUALITY BOOKS
IN BOTH PRINT AND ELECTRONIC FORMATS

ACTION/ADVENTURE

SCIENCE FICTION

MAINSTREAM

FANTASY

ROMANCE

HISTORICAL

YOUNG ADULT

SUSPENSE/THRILLER

PARANORMAL

MYSTERY

EROTICA

HORROR

WESTERN

NON-FICTION

AMBER QUILL PRESS, LLC
http://www.amberquill.com

759336

Made in the USA